Twisted

J.L. Meyrick

To Honey

Gnjoy!

Jh Meyrick

To my new husband, James, who made sure I sat down to write.

To Cat, who wouldn't stop prodding me to write this book.

Contents

Preface

To any of my family reading this book. If you wish to skip the more detailed aspects of a romance novel, then don't read the italicised section of chapter eighteen!

Chapter One

Imagine a world full of people, special people, people who hardly seemed human. That's our world: a world of heroes, people who have extraordinary powers. Unfortunately, in a world with heroes, you also have a world with villains.

The latest battle of Good vs Evil took place late last night across the city. Crashing from building to park to civil offices.

However, the damage could have been a lot worse if it weren't for the hard work of our national hero.

A loud crash brought Liliana out of the narrative she was writing. She heard a moan from the floor. Looking down, she saw an intern sprawled across the thin excuse for a carpet the facilities team tried to pass by them.

"Are you okay down there?" she asked, pushing back from her desk to help the poor boy up.

"Oh, uh, yeah." He cleared his throat as he scrambled to his feet. "I mean, yes, thank you. I lost my footing there for a moment. I'm sorry to disturb you." He seemed nervous and possibly annoyed at himself.

"No, no, it's okay. Is this your first day or something?" she asked, trying to help the boy calm down.

"Is it that obvious?" he replied, brushing his hand through his shaggy hair. "This chance is all I've wanted for years now, and here I am, falling over my own feet on my first day. What a smart impression I'm giving."

Liliana laughed slightly at his nervousness. "Oh, this is nothing. You've not seen true embarrassment yet."

"What? Was your day worse?" He raised his eyebrows, expecting to hear some terribly embarrassing story.

"Well, not my first day." Liliana turned to call over the cubicle to the opposite desk. "Rose! Tell this kid about your first day, would you?"

A tall redhead shot up, her face quickly matching her fiery locks. "No! You promised you wouldn't mention that anymore!" she exclaimed, half angry, half ashamed. Liliana's laughter grew at her response. She loved to tease Rose. Rose's pale pink cheeks darkened with a blush of embarrassment. "Don't you dare, Lil, or I'll tell him about your twenty-fifth birthday."

The threat shut Liliana up quickly. "You wouldn't." She locked eyes with Rose for a moment before the two smiled at each other and turned back to the intern.

"Don't worry, kid. Everyone has a bad day now and then, you got yours out of the way early. Smart," Rose said, calming him down. "What's your name, anyway?"

"Johnathon."

"Well, Johnny, welcome to The Daylight Observer. Liliana and I are always happy to keep an eye out for the newbies, so come to us with any questions you have." Rose was the mother hen of the office and she had the fierce side to prove it. If she took anyone in under her wing, they were well protected. Even the managers were unwilling to go toe-to-toe with her on minor issues.

"Thanks. It's nice to know people here are so friendly," Johnathon replied, happy to have made some friends on his first day.

"Ms Masters!" a loud voice shouted down the hallway and to the group of cubicles where they were standing. A tall woman followed the voice. White power suit, sharp blonde bob, and a frown to complete the ensemble. "Where is the latest battle piece I requested?" she asked, a little too loudly to be polite.

"I'm just finishing it up now," Liliana replied, almost standing to attention. You couldn't help but straighten your back in the presence of Tanya Netting, the fearsome editor-in-chief, like she was a drill sergeant and you a green recruit.

"Have you developed a new power we don't know about?" Tanya replied, confusing Liliana.

"Power, Ma'am?"

"Yes. I didn't realise you could write and socialise at the same time," she replied, sarcasm dripping from her voice at every syllable.

"Right. Yes, ma'am. I'll get the article sent to you right away." Liliana darted back to her desk and started typing as she spoke. Liliana went from frightened and pale to a flushed tawny as she realised Tanya was trying to make a joke. Not her strongest trait.

"You, intern! Follow me."

Johnathon looked like a deer in headlights as he stumbled after Tanya.

"Poor lad won't last the day with the witch," Rose whispered over the cubicle divider.

Liliana chuckled as she finished the article she'd been working on and sent it over to the witch in question. Turning over to her emails to check in with the world, she glanced at the picture on her desk, the one personal item Tanya allowed each person to have. A picture of herself standing in front of a local fountain, curled into a tall, dark-haired, brown-skinned man. Her man. Her Max.

They'd been together for nearly a year now, it'd been a fast-moving, passionate year. What had been an accidental bump in the paper's corridors had spun into the most exciting relationship she'd had.

PING.

Her email alert drew her attention back to her computer. It was from Max. Liliana took a glance around, making sure Tanya wasn't anywhere nearby before opening the email.

Hello, love,

I'm afraid I need to push back our plans for this evening. I'm about to go into a meeting that could last awhile. Can we meet at 8 instead of 7? Still at Graciano's, they've agreed to move our reservation.

All my love,

Max.

Liliana hit reply.

Of course, that's fine by me. I can't wait!

See you at 8.

Love always,

Liliana.

She'd been waiting for months to go to Graciano's. It was the newest hit restaurant in the city, with a waiting list of six months. She supposed that was the benefit of dating a man like Max; he opened doors previously closed to her. That wasn't the reason she was dating him. She never set out to date a millionaire. Not even her parents expected that to happen. They were thrilled with her match. Not that they were entirely thrilled with all her life choices.

They didn't want their only daughter to become a journalist. No, they'd hoped for a doctor or a lawyer. Something like that. Once they'd realised Liliana wanted to become a journalist they'd thrown themselves into researching what heights a journalist could reach. They started nagging Liliana to reach these near-impossible heights. Where was her Pulitzer? Why wasn't she promoted to an editor yet? Why didn't she have her own office?

It wasn't like she was still relatively new to the field; she was only twenty-eight, still plenty of time to achieve all those things. Her parents were never happy with her. But she did her best not to think about it unless they were actively interrogating her.

Max was completely different. He appreciated her for who she was. He encouraged her to follow her dreams of being an accomplished journalist. They had long discussions on current affairs, issues with superheroes and what they do. He gave her new ideas to write about through these discussions, angles she might not have thought about before. Any discussion with him about the issues the world was facing turned into a new article idea for her. They also gave him new ideas to take to his business. He wanted to help the world through his technology. Liliana admired that about him. He wasn't like a lot of rich people who only wanted to make more money, regardless of the method. He was always looking for a way to improve life for the people in the city and beyond.

Of course, it did help that he was extremely good looking. The tabloids loved to take pictures of him out and about the city. Liliana wasn't normally the vain type who only went by appearance, but damn, he looked good. She'd quite enjoyed their time together. From the start there was a spark. That spark swiftly grew into a passionate encounter.

She stopped scrolling through her emails as her mind jumped back to their first night together. Candles lit the room, sweet scents filled the air. Max had wide, open windows leading out to a view over the city. Close enough to appreciate the lights of the living city, but far enough for a decent amount of privacy. Hands on skin, breath on the back of her neck as she looked out over the city.

"Nice view, isn't it?" Max whispered behind her, handing her a glass of water.

"Lovely. It's like you're above the city, watching people go about their lives completely unaware of you. Feels powerful." She took a sip of water before placing it down on the side table.

Max chuckled. "I see it more like I can watch over the people. Not that they need me, they have the heroes for that, I suppose. But I like to feel like I can help them."

"I like it when you talk all philanthropic," Liliana whispered, turning around to face his six-foot-four frame. She wrapped her arms around his muscular torso. Liliana smiled up at him. She breathed in his warm scent as he brought her close. The air got warmer between them as Max brought her lips upward to meet his.

"MS MASTERS!" A shout brought Liliana out of her memory rather sharply. She jumped almost out of her seat and saw Tanya stood next to her desk. "I do not appreciate having to repeat myself."

"Yes. Sorry, Ma'am. I'm with you now." A different sort of heat rose as Liliana's face turned beetroot red.

"I said you need to head out to Central Plaza. I need you to cover the speech. Get your head out of the clouds and your shit together." She was pissed and the entire office knew it. Heads were poking up over the cubicles like meerkats from their burrows. "If you would rather be anywhere else, I can fill your position with a snap of my fingers." Tanya held up her hand as a threat.

"No, Ma'am, I love my job. I apologise. My mind distracted me for a moment. It won't happen again." Liliana chucked her notebook and pen in her bag and stood next to Tanya. An arch appeared in Tanya's eyebrow as she stared Liliana down for a moment.

Liliana could feel her hands twitching with nerves, her heart pounding against her chest, breath catching in her throat. She didn't break contact with Tanya's piercing blue eyes, eyes that would look lovely on a pleasant person's face. Liliana's brown eyes wanted to look anywhere else. What felt like an eternity later, Tanya blinked.

"Fine. Go."

Liliana relaxed her dry eyes, letting out a sigh of relief. She glanced over at Rose who stood after Tanya had marched back to her corner office.

"Jesus Christ, that woman needs to relax. Are you okay?"

"I'm fine. Just need to stop my heart racing a mile a minute," Liliana laughed nervously. "I better get going. Do you know what speech she was talking about?" She felt like she'd missed something, which, considering she worked in journalism, wasn't a wonderful thing to do.

"The Mayor has just announced that he's giving an emergency speech at the Plaza this afternoon. Word just came down. Something big is happening. I'll come with you, get some pictures for your coverage." Rose grabbed her camera bag and they walked through the office together.

Liliana could feel eyes watching her as she walked. While someone got shouted at daily here, it wasn't often that loud or dramatic.

"Bloody Max," Liliana whispered under her breath. He had a nasty habit of distracting her at work.

"What was that?" Rose asked, smirking.

"Nothing."

"Got a certain dark-haired hunk on your mind?"

"I'm sure I don't know what you mean," Liliana couldn't help but laugh. She relaxed; Rose always knew how to calm her down after an encounter with the she-devil.

Chapter Two

The two headed out to the elevator, laughing together. Jumping into a cab outside of the office, the two friends shared their thoughts on what the speech could be about.

"A new crime fighting initiative?" Liliana posed.

"Or a collaboration with a new hero?" Rose replied.

"Or maybe he's resigning? His numbers haven't been great recently," Liliana wondered.

"Oh, that's possible. A resignation speech would be good for you. Might get Tanya off your back for a while."

"I heard an old bad guy is back on the scene," a voice called back from the front of the cab; the driver had been listening to them speculate.

"Where did you hear that?" Rose asked.

"Oh, just another of my passengers." The driver waved his hand as he took a left-hand turn towards the Plaza. His tone betrayed nothing of his emotions. He seemed bored, like he needed another supervillain just to shake up his daily routine.

Rose turned to Liliana, raising her eyebrow, as if to say, "Sure, that sounds credible." They always had an uncanny ability to understand each other without the use of words. It's what made them a wonderful couple for a while there. Friends turned to lovers; they were unstoppable. Rose always knew what to do with Liliana. They were in love for a time. But they made better friends.

Rose was supportive of Liliana and Max when they first started seeing each other, even making the introductions. If you even needed proper introductions after literally running into each other. Rose had been doing an interview with him for their summer expo on business leaders in the city. He walked out of the private room just as Liliana was running past to the print room. Normally, she wasn't the clumsy type. But when you're running, you don't have as much time to switch trajectory as you need. Max tried to catch her, but she fell flat on her backside. She could still feel the bruise all this time later.

She still remembered looking at Max for the first time from her perspective on the floor. She was a little annoyed, to be honest. A little at herself for falling, a bit more at the man who didn't look where he was going when he entered a busy newsroom. But his concerned smile as he held out his hand to help her up would stay with her for a while.

"Here we are, the Plaza. Looks kinda busy, don't

you think?" the driver called back to Liliana and Rose in the backseat. They glanced out of the window to the sea of paparazzi and reporters surrounding a stage in the centre of the square. There was a curtained area at the back, presumably hiding the Mayor from sight before his announcement.

Liliana's heart raced and her fingers twitched as she stepped out of the cab. Looking back at Rose, she could tell she was also worrying about what the speech could be about to call this many people so quickly. Sure, the news was fast in the city, but this was taking it a step further than either of them had seen before.

Her breath caught at the back of her throat as she entered the crowd, pressure on her shoulder as Rose used her cool hand to keep them together. They made their way through the crowd to the area that was roped off for the larger local news companies. Briefly, she felt grateful for having the special access that her ID card allowed her. Until she saw who they were sharing their space with.

A tall, pale, dark-haired man stood at the front of their roped off area, a familiar bag slung over his shoulder and a notebook already half filled in his perfectly manicured hands. Tim, lead political reporter for The Daily Tribune, Liliana's chief opponent in their field. Arrogance needed no other poster boy. He stood at six foot-two and behaved as if he had earned every inch above her admittedly short five-foot-two frame. True, he had been in the field for longer than her, but was twelve months worth the tension between them?

"Ah, Ana, nice to see you again," Tim drawled as he noticed his new company.

"I told you not to call me that again, Timmy," she replied, curt yet calm. She didn't feel calm, she never did around Tim. He always set her on edge, regardless of words spoken.

Tim chuckled at her reply and turned back to his notebook. Liliana tried to sneak a peek out of the corner of her eye, but his handwriting was atrocious. Impossible for her to decipher without closer examination.

"I'll show you mine if you show me yours," Tim said, clearly noticing her spy attempt.

"Excuse me?" Rose asked, unaware of what was going on.

"Your friend here was trying to read my notes. I was simply offering an exchange of information."

"Mhm, sure." Rose raised her brow as she pulled out her equipment from the overlarge bag she brought with her, setting up a tripod ready for the speech. Liliana turned to help her with the setup. "Just ignore him, Lil, he's not worth it." She wasn't sure if Rose meant that for Liliana or for herself. Rose seemed to blow up at Tim more often than Liliana did, so it wasn't just her that didn't like the pompous asshole.

The surrounding crowd was getting louder as the group waited for the speech to begin. Suddenly, it didn't just seem to be the press present. Members of the public surrounded the reporters. Some seemed intrigued, but some seemed unhappy. With what? Liliana wasn't sure, but she didn't like the look on some of their faces. She was unsettled to see the lack of security in the Plaza, especially because the Mayor was about to go on stage in front of a rather large, and loud, crowd of people.

Slowly, a noise came through louder than the crowd, a chant carrying over the sea of reporters. Liliana couldn't quite make it out yet. She turned to Rose, brows furrowed in worry.

"This is going to get interesting, isn't it?" She took a step closer to Rose, as if to gain better protection from her friend.

"Do you think they are pro or con? Is the Mayor in danger from this? I hope the Supers are on standby."

"Why aren't the police here? There isn't any proper security!" Liliana disliked the Mayor's apparent refusal to utilise the police. He much preferred the superheroes that protected the city. "He shouldn't rely on the heroes so much. They aren't always available, surely they lead their own lives."

"What's wrong with relying on the Supers? Isn't that the point of them? They're here to protect us, to keep us safe from the bad guys."

If there was any position Liliana and Rose disagreed on, it was the Supers. While Liliana was grateful for the work they'd done for the city over the last ten years, they were the exception, not the rule. People couldn't trust them to be there every time or there would be no crime, no danger. They couldn't trust heroes. Rose essentially just wanted to do trust falls with them all the time. She was losing her sense of danger, of self-preservation. She would always tell new people about the time Sentinel saved her life. A getaway vehicle was about to crash into her. Thankfully, he arrived just at the right time.

"Well, we will never agree about the Supers, Rose. Though I do hope they are around, I'd rather not be in the middle of a riot or anything today. That's getting a little too close to the news for me."

Liliana heard a chuckle to her side. "Yes, Tim?"

"No, don't worry," he sighed. "It's cute, really. You don't like the Supers, but you're happy for them to help when you need them. They're not here just for you, you know that right?"

"Of course, I do. Just because I don't agree with how people treat them, doesn't mean I can't appreciate what they do." Liliana was getting to the end of her tether with Tim, to be honest. Why did they have to be paired together in the press section? The organiser clearly wasn't aware of their history together.

"Sure," Tim drawled, looking down on her. Liliana looked back at Rose, sharing a look meaning that Liliana was one step away from launching herself at Tim.

"Lils! There you are!" a voice called over her inner monologue planning out what she would like to do with Tim if she were truly able. Her heart jumped as she heard the voice that both calmed her down and got her all riled up, differently, all in one go.

"Max! What are you doing here?" Liliana let him into the private area, feeling much more comfortable with him standing next to her.

"Hi there, handsome," Rose said, looking Max up and down.

"Calm down, Rose, you know I'm taken," Max joked. Liliana loved their relationship. If another woman heard what they said to each other, they'd think something was going on between them. Of course, it helped to know that Rose was gay. She was more likely to steal Liliana than Max.

"Shame. I'll repeat what our girl here said. What are you doing here?"

"Hi, love," Max dropped a quick kiss on Liliana's soft lips. "Same as you guys, I suppose. I want to know what the Mayor is going to say. It could impact some work I'm doing." Max looped his arm around Liliana's waist, pulling her gently towards his side as he spotted Tim over the top of her head. "Mr. Westfield, I hope you are keeping well." Polite, yet curt at the same time. Max shared Liliana's opinion of Tim since long before they bumped into each other, apparently.

"Max, how are you?" Tim replied, trying to seem friendly. Max ignored him and turned back to Liliana, who gave him a small smile. She loved it when he saw Tim, he said what she couldn't. Professional courtesy always got in her way. She could hear Tim cluck his tongue as he made yet more notes in his book.

"It shouldn't be long. The Mayor's scheduled to go on in a minute or two. Are we all set up, Rose?" Liliana asked.

"Yep, camera's ready to go. Do you need anything else?"

Liliana made sure she switched on the Dictaphone, ready to record, and her own notebook was open, pen ready.

Max leaned in behind her as she got herself ready. "I love to see you work," he whispered in her ear, hands relaxing on her hips. She felt the heat rising in her body as she turned to say something. Before the words could leave her mouth, her lips were rather busy being brushed up against Max's.

"Come on, people. While we are outside, this is a workspace!" Rose called over the sound of Liliana's heart beating in her ears. Max pulled away, giving her a smirk. He knew what he was doing. She lightly smacked his arm and turned back towards the stage just as a hush came over the crowd. The Mayor was walking up the steps to the left of the microphone.

"Welcome, and thank you all for joining me on such short notice. I know you all have busy lives, so I will get down to business. In response to the latest in a long line of Powered battles yesterday, the Council and I have agreed to formalise a superhero implementation policy." Liliana was furiously scribbling in her notebook, the clicking of the cameras around her spurring her on. She was vaguely aware of Max standing next to her, murmuring to himself. He didn't seem happy with the way the speech was going. The crowds of the public surrounding the press built their momentum again. Liliana couldn't tell if it was to support the Mayor or not.

"Several of the Supers have approached me in the last couple of weeks regarding a Taskforce made up of Powered individuals. A Taskforce that would serve the public office to improve the interests of the public. After intense discussion with the Council, we came to the agreement to install a formal Taskforce made up of these Powered individuals."

Max was murmuring more under his breath, clearly getting angrier and angrier with the Mayor. Liliana glanced away from her notebook. She had never seen him so angry in their relationship. She half expected him to call out to the Mayor suddenly.

"This Taskforce will be in charge of city security on the large scale, as well as partially focused on crime prevention," the Mayor continued, detailing his plan for the new Taskforce. Liliana could tell this was going to be the story of the year, splitting the city down the middle. She feared for what would happen when the two sides met.

Liliana continued scribbling in her notebook furiously, trying to keep up with the Mayor's speech. Pain shot from her fingers, up to her elbow, as her hand cramped up. Soon, she would have to stop and rely on her recording of the event. The clicking of the camera beside her kept her at a steady pace. The Mayor seemed to just be rounding out his speech when he made the mistake of asking for questions. Suddenly, the surrounding crowd started shouting their questions.

"Where is the budget for this Taskforce coming from?"

"Which Supers are a part of the Taskforce?"

"Why now? Why not before all this crime got out of hand?"

Liliana didn't bother trying to make herself heard over the crowd. She was too far back from the stage to stand a chance. At least, that was what she thought before Max spoke out.

"How can you expect the public to learn self-preservation if you mollycoddle them like this?" he boomed out, silencing those around him. Max stood to his full height and stared the Mayor down.

"Ah, Max, good to see you again," the Mayor replied, resigned as he realised who had asked the question. Liliana felt a different type of heat rising as half the live feed cameras turned to focus on Max during the back and forth about to happen.

"And to see you, Mr. Mayor," Max replied, waiting for his answer. The Mayor sighed before adjusting his glasses. He seemed to brace himself before the coming storm.

"It is not mollycoddling as you so crudely put it. I am simply keeping my constituents' best interests at heart. I want to keep them safe; this is the best way to do so." The Mayor was confident in his answer, sure he had shut Max up. Unfortunately for him, he didn't know Max as well as he thought he did.

"Not letting them deal with their own issues, or develop their own backbone, is not in their best interests, Mr. Mayor. Neither is reducing the local police stations to the point of making them security guards. This policy will lead to massive job losses in the authority's sector. What will you do about that?" Max kept his words even-tempered, but Liliana could tell he was getting himself worked up.

"The police force will still have plenty of work to do—"

"Yeah, handing out parking tickets."

"—the Powered Taskforce will simply take care of the most dangerous situations, the ones that put our hardworking police officers in real danger."

"And who will draw that line? You? The Supers?" Max clenched his fists, frustrated with the Mayor's apparent lack of concern for his issues.

"I think that will be all for questions today. Thank you all for coming." The Mayor scampered off the stage after Max's last question. Clearly, he didn't want the public to wonder who was really in charge of this new Taskforce. Max stared after the Mayor's retreating backside. He wanted to get a few more shots in before he backed down.

"Max, are you okay?" Liliana brushed her hand against Max's arm, bringing him out of his stare down with fresh air.

"I'm fine, love, you don't need to worry about me. The Mayor will listen to sense one day soon, I'm sure of it." Max was quiet, focused. Honestly, it scared Liliana a little. He was normally quite care-free and smiley. Now, he was calm, but with a bit of resting bitch face.

"I need to get back to the office and get this written up, pronto. Are you going to be okay on your own?" Liliana worried about what Max was going to do.

She'd never seen him like this before.

"I'll be okay. Yates is back at the car waiting for me. I have some business to take care of this afternoon before our dinner tonight." Max rolled his shoulders, relieving the tension he'd been holding. He stooped to plant a kiss on Liliana's cheek before turning to walk towards the closest car park.

"Nice interrogation," an arrogant voice called over, his tone conveying that he didn't appreciate the questions Max had shot at the Mayor.

"Not now, Tim, leave us alone," Liliana called back before Max could respond. He still turned to stare Tim down, who didn't seem fazed by the glare at all. The two looked to be facing off for a moment before Tim packed up his gear and walked off.

"That guy seriously bothers me," Max muttered to Liliana and Rose before waving goodbye.

"Is Max okay?" Rose asked under her breath after packing up her camera.

"I'm not sure. He isn't usually like that. The Supers are a bit of a sore topic for him, though." Liliana pondered Max's motivations internally. She hoped he'd be calmer by their dinner tonight.

The pair made their way back to the office as quickly as possible; their cab driver was, thankfully, a lot quieter than their last. Liliana spent the quick trip running over her notes, already composing her article in her mind, ready to send over to

Tanya who would surely want it done by yesterday. Rose was just as focused, clicking through her plethora of pictures from the short yet powerful speech.

Tanya was waiting for them outside of the elevator on their floor of the news building. That was never a good sign. She marched them to their desks. "I saw the live footage. What have you got for me?"

"I'll have the finished article in your inbox in twenty minutes. Rose has an excellent selection of photos for you as well."

"They just need a quick touch-up and they'll be ready for the evening news."

"Forget the evening news, I want the piece online as soon as possible." She clicked her fingers as if the finished article would appear in her hands. "Make it fifteen minutes, and it better be perfect," she demanded before storming off to editorial.

Liliana and Rose shared a brief look before getting down to work. The surrounding office was abuzz with the news of the new Taskforce. The other reporters were looking at it from every viewpoint while Liliana was covering the speech itself. She wondered if there would be any space in the evening paper for anything else to be reported.

Ten short minutes later, she had the speech coverage sent over to the she-devil for her to pick apart until nothing remained. It was in moments like this that she both loved and hated her job. The fast pace kept her on her toes, and she was continually developing her reporting skills. But the stress, combined with feeling like she was simply a viewer sitting on the side of history, got to her sometimes. She wanted to feel like she had done something with her life, instead of just reporting on other people's lives. If she were honest, she felt stuck, unsure of what to do next with her life.

Liliana shook herself out of her thoughts. There was no point going down that road. It wasn't like she could do anything about it anyway. She was happy where she was, her family was happy, and she was practically successful. So that was it. She was going to continue working at the paper, eventually making her way up the company, and she'd retire comfortably. Liliana had her life planned out long ago. So why didn't it feel right?

Chapter Three

"Johnny, there you are. Come with me, we're going to get coffee." Rose nabbed the intern as he was rushing past their desks.

"But we have a machine in the kitchen, don't we?" His brow furrowed.

"That swill? You'll learn to avoid it soon enough, lad, don't you worry."

"Wait up, I'll come with you." Liliana needed a screen break. She jogged to catch up with the pair as they were leaving the office.

"Do you guys get to leave the office for coffee often, then? It doesn't feel right to me." Johnathon was skittish, typical new starter nerves.

"Tanya doesn't mind if you bring her back a latte. If you come back empty-handed though, duck and cover!" Liliana replied. "She knows we work best while caffeine-fuelled, so she ignores our absences."

"Oh, okay, if you're sure."

"How are you finding your first day? You picked the right day for it," Rose asked, sure he was on the edge of some sort of breakdown.

"Is it normally like this?"

"Not usually. The Mayor doesn't have a habit of announcing ground-breaking policies regularly," Liliana replied sarcastically.

"True, I suppose. It's a madhouse up there. I don't know how you work so quickly. I don't think I'm cut out for this." The boy was getting himself worked up to a panic attack before the elevator reached the bottom floor.

"Relax, Johnny, take a deep breath for me. Try to calm your breathing," Rose spoke over him, getting and maintaining eye contact, trying to head off the panic before it kicked in. They were breathing together as the doors to the elevator opened to the lobby. Liliana held back the people waiting to get on the elevator for a moment until Johnathon seemed calm enough to get moving. Unfortunately, this wasn't exactly an uncommon occurrence in a news building. Stress levels were at an all-time high, people broke occasionally. Liliana questioned her life choices again until Rose and Johnathon brought her out of it by walking past her. Giving herself a little shake, she caught up and left the building with her friends.

Crossing the street, they walked into their closest independent coffee shop. Liliana and Rose were regular enough. The staff recognised them and started their order before they could get to the counter.

"Not so busy today, Carl?" Liliana asked over the counter to the short, round man making their coffees.

"Ah, it's not been too bad. Had a rush after the speech but most of 'em were in and out," Carl replied, expertly pouring coffee and milk into to-go cups. "Anything new for you today?" he asked, nodding to Johnathon.

"Oh, I'll just have a black coffee, please," Johnathon replied.

"Comin' right up."

Rose tapped her card on the reader, paying for the four drinks. Liliana loved it in the coffee shop. She got a view of the variety of lives lived in the surrounding city. Old and young, rich and not so rich. They all came into this shop. Excellent coffee at low prices would always bring in plenty of customers. There was a small area at the back of the shop where you could sit in plush chairs and read an assortment of books Carl kept for his customers to peruse.

"Oh, that's excellent coffee," Johnathon commented, sipping it as soon as he got it.

"Johnny! Isn't that scalding hot?" Liliana exclaimed.

"Oh right, yeah, it's hot. Don't worry," Johnathon froze, realising what he just did. "I'm okay. Let's get

Tanya her latte, should we? Don't want to keep her waiting." He grabbed the latte and headed straight for the door, ignoring the shocked looks on everybody's faces. Sharing a quick look of astonishment, Liliana and Rose ran after him.

They were about to follow him across the street when Rose pulled Liliana back hard enough to make her drop her cappuccino. "Rose, what was that for?" she shouted, just as a car door went flying past where she was about to walk. Looking to their right, they spotted something they never hoped to see in person. A fight, but not just any fight, a Super fight.

"Oh crap. We need to run, now!" Liliana grabbed Rose's hand and ran back into the coffee shop behind them. "Carl! Get everyone out the back door. Something big is going down, down the street. We need to get to safety."

For such a small, round man, Carl was a quick mover. "You heard her people! Get those asses in gear and out the back!" He shepherded his customers through the kitchen to the back alley.

"Thank you, Rose. You saved my life there," Liliana gasped as she half ran behind Carl.

"Did you see who that was? That was Sentinel fighting!" Rose was starstruck. One would remember the man who saved your life.

"Yeah, I saw. I also saw the car door that would have sliced me in half. We need to keep moving, we aren't invulnerable, Rose. We could get really hurt if we get caught up in this." Liliana's heart was thudding in her chest, so much she was sure it was visible.

Sunlight blinded them as they came out of the back door of the coffee shop. Carl was still shepherding his customers down the alley that led to the next street.

"Keep going people, head for the subway. It isn't far from here. We'll be safe soon, don't you worry." He had taken control of the situation like a pro. Liliana wondered if he had been in this kind of situation before. He was staying remarkably calm. Liliana was laser focused on keeping herself and Rose safe. She could stress about it later.

"Did you see who Sentinel was fighting? I swear he looked familiar," Rose asked, still watching the fight rather than running for their lives.

"Familiar? You glimpsed the bad guy from half a block away. He couldn't have been that familiar." She was getting annoyed with Rose. Why couldn't she see the danger they were in?

The group rounded the corner from the alley to the street as they felt a rumble that knocked a few runners to the ground. The ground rumbled again, pursued by a deafening boom and crash. Liliana didn't want to know what was causing it, she just wanted to get away from the fighting. Stooping to help up those who had fallen, Liliana spotted the entry to the subway twenty feet away. The fastest of the group were already descending the stairs, lost in a crowd of people also on the run.

Liliana took a quick glance back towards the news building. She saw some windows were smashed, including some on her floor. She was suddenly very glad for coffee. She saw Sentinel fly around the edge of her building; he was being chased by a figure in what looked like a suit of armour. But he was flying as well. That didn't look easy in a metal suit.

Hang on. Sentinel was flying away from the suit-man? Why would he try to escape? He was the most powerful of all the Supers; he feared nothing. Liliana watched them fight for a moment. The dynamic made little sense to her. Why were they flying around the news building? Most big fights took place in open areas, not around high rises, they're too dangerous. At the very least, Sentinel should try to get the suitman out of the city. Instead, he was leading him towards her building.

Before she could figure it out, she noticed Sentinel fire on the building, narrowly missing the suit-man. The blast took out a sizeable chunk of the building, exposing the steel poles running up the middle of the construction.

Liliana sucked in a sharp breath. It stung her chest and burned her throat as she watched her office being destroyed. If she hadn't left for coffee, she'd be dead.

"Oh my god. Did you see that? Sentinel almost had him!" Rose exclaimed next to her.

"Did YOU see that? He just took out our office. When does Sentinel miss? Or fight in the middle of the city? Something is going on here, Rose." Liliana was panicking. She couldn't catch her breath and her heart was trying to escape her chest.

Carl grabbed her arm and pulled her down to the subway, cramming them into the crowds. Terrified people shoved, nudged, and knocked her so much, Liliana lost sight of Rose in the mix.

"Rose!" she called, trying to see over the heads of those surrounding her. Cries of fear filled the air as crashing booms continued above them. It was in this moment she really hated being as short as she was. Shoulders knocked her about so much her head was hurting. "Rose! Where are you?" She fought through the crowd as best as she could as she heard a faint voice calling her name.

"Liliana! Liliana!" Rose was calling her from some-where to her left. Liliana turned, shouting back, trying to push past the masses. Elbows were dig-ging into her ribs and arms, bruises soon to follow. Deafening booms continued above them, screams followed shortly after each one. Dust was shaking down onto panicked heads. It sounded like they were fighting right above them now. Liliana half expected them to come crashing through the ceiling onto them.

"Rose!" Liliana glimpsed Rose not far ahead of her. She looked as worried as Liliana felt. They stretched out their hands to grab onto each other just as an elbow came out of nowhere and hit Liliana in the head. The world went dark as Liliana fell to the floor.

Chapter Four

She was floating in nothing. It was comfortable and terrifying all at the same time. Liliana didn't know what was happening, or what had just happened before the floating sensation. Were her eyes open? She couldn't see anything but that could just be the back of her eyelids for all she knew. Was she dreaming? Was she dead? That thought should have scared her more than it did. She was oddly calm, calmer than she had ever been before. It was nice.

She was happily floating in nothing when she felt a gentle tug pulling her down. Suddenly, she had a sense of which way was up. Ever so slowly, she felt herself falling and straightening up so she was standing. Finally, she felt solid ground under her bare feet, though she couldn't tell what the sensation was. A dim light formed in front of her. She knew now that her eyes were closed as the light shone through her eyelids. Blinking slowly, she opened her eyes to see a familiar scene. Why was it familiar?

She saw a room, a soft rug under her feet, a cosy

chair sat in front of her behind a small desk. She curled her toes into the rug. Feeling the soft fibres scrunch up, she took a deep breath in and noticed a familiar scent. Again, unaware of why it was familiar. It was a comfortable, relaxing home. Home? Was this her home? That seemed right. This was her room, her study, where she worked.

Looking behind her, she saw through the open door to her main living space. She walked through to see her couch, well used, draped in blankets and cushions. Across from the couch was her television and gaming system. She spent many hours here relaxing after a hard day's work. She saw another open door and heard a rustling on the other side. Before she could explore further, a person walked through into the living room.

"Max," Liliana sighed, smiling at the man she loved. She felt unable to move towards him.

Max stopped short of arm's length in front of Liliana. He had a confused smile spread across his face; calm but worried eyes gazed at her.

"Max? What's wrong?" Liliana struggled to keep ahold of the calm feeling she craved.

"I'm sorry, Lils." His eyes watered. She had never seen him cry before.

"What do you mean? What could you be sorry for?" Liliana worried, the calm feeling long gone.

"I should have told you. I should have been honest.

I'm sorry—"

She jolted backwards, cutting Max off. Something pulled her out of her home, back through the space. Max held out his hand as something pulled her away, the vision of her happy place shrinking quickly. She felt a sudden hardness at her back, hot air pressing down on her.

"Liliana!" a voice cried above her. Liliana was aware she was now lying on something hard. Confusion briefly consumed her before her memories of before rushed back at her. She sat up swiftly, gasping for air. Hands on her shoulder, keeping her steady.

"Liliana! Finally, you're awake." Rose's face swam into view before Liliana. "Are you okay? You hit your head quite hard there," Rose worried, clearly holding back panic and horror in her clenched jaw.

"Ow. Oh god, that hurts." Liliana grabbed her head; she hadn't noticed the pain until Rose mentioned it. The ground began to spin beneath her. Holding back the urge to throw up, her throat burned. "What's happening? How long was I out?"

"It's been about ten minutes. I can't hear anymore fighting, I think it's over. No one here will go look though." Liliana nodded her sore head. She decided they should be the ones to look if no one else would. "Can you stand?" Rose asked. Liliana nodded again, immediately regretting it. She took in a deep breath before drawing her feet under her.

Rose helped her up slowly, the ground still spinning a little under her. As soon as she got upright, her legs shook. The ground beneath her didn't seem stable enough to be walking on. She was about to fall when a hand grabbed her elbow. Rose was keeping her upright.

"I got you, don't worry."

"Love you, Rose." Liliana lent her head on Rose's shoulder as they made their way to the subway entrance, hoping not to hear anymore crashes above them. Instead, they heard sirens blaring around the city above them. Oddly, that reassured them. If the emergency services were out and about, that would mean the immediate danger had passed.

Liliana had never found a set of stairs to look so daunting. Then again, she had never passed out before. Step by step, it felt like she was climbing Mount Everest going up these fifteen steps. She lent into Rose as much as she could as the steps moved underneath her. One, two, three, these steps were never ending.

Sunlight burst over the top step, blinding Liliana and Rose as they struggled up into the world. Sirens blared all around them, the noise filling the city. Lights flashed past them, heading back towards the news building.

Liliana fought back the urge to hurl her breakfast across the street in front of her. She saw smoke in the distance, across the city. The fight had clearly taken its toll on the skyline. Her building was no different. It looked on the brink of collapse. She couldn't see her apartment building from here, but she hoped it remained intact.

"We should get you to the hospital."

"No. No, I'm okay, I'm—" She stumbled over her own feet and scraped her knee on the pavement before Rose could catch her.

"Ow." Liliana clutched her knee as Rose hurled her back up to standing. "Okay, maybe I need to get checked over. Why can't I stay balanced? Why do I need to throw up so badly?" The world and everything in it confused her right now.

"All bets on a concussion, Lils." Rose's attention seemed split between keeping Liliana upright and moving, and searching for something. What she was searching for, Liliana wasn't sure.

"Where is he?" Rose mumbled to herself, eyes scanning the sky above them.

"Who?"

"What?" Rose looked back at Liliana, not understanding that she had heard her mumbling. "Come on, the hospital is around the corner here. Let's get you checked over." Rose was trying to distract her. They stumbled around the corner to spot a rush of people moving in and out of the hospital.

They pushed past people, clamouring for attention from the nurses and receptionists who stood at the doors trying to direct people.

One nurse stood with a megaphone, shouting over the masses.

"If your injuries are critical, please follow the red line to your right, we will see you immediately. If your injuries are serious but not life-threatening, please follow the amber line to triage. Someone will see you as soon as possible. If your injuries are minor, please follow the green line to the waiting room where you will be seen when possible. If you can self-treat your injuries, please do. This includes scrapes and bruises, NOT broken bones or cuts requiring stitches." Several nurses were inspecting people unsure of what line they needed to follow.

Rose and Liliana shuffled for a few minutes until they could speak to a nurse directing people.

"My friend hit her head. She was unconscious. I think she might have a concussion." As if to aid Rose's description of her injuries, Liliana's legs went out from underneath her as she blacked out for the second time that day.

Chapter Five

Images flashed through Liliana's mind as she once again tried to figure out what was happening to her. Fluorescent lights passed over her. She was moving somehow. A blinding light flashed over her eyes, followed by a glimpse of a woman wearing a mask and gloves. Where was she? The answer felt like it was just out of reach.

A splash of red hair appeared above her, worried eyes on the brink of tears. Her mouth moved to form words Liliana couldn't understand. She wanted to comfort the redhead. Rose! The redhead was called Rose; she was a friend. With that realisation, the rest flooded back into her mind. She was in the hospital; she'd passed out again after hitting her head earlier.

What felt like only seconds later, Liliana opened her eyes to see a hospital room. She was on a bed, hooked up to several monitors. Her head felt tight, like a boa constrictor had her in its grip. Just as the pain was about to reach a crescendo, a wave of cold flushed up her arm. She looked down to see they'd hooked her up to a drip filled with what seemed to be painkillers. A breath of relief loosened up her tense muscles. She hadn't even noticed how tense she was till she relaxed back into the bed.

"Lils? You awake? How are you feeling?" Rose stood up from the hard wooden chair at the side of the room. She took Liliana's hand gently as she waited for her to speak.

Liliana put her other hand to her head to end the throbbing. She felt something wrapped around her forehead, a bandage by the feel.

"They had to give you some stitches. You had a nasty cut on the side of your head. The bandage is to stop you from itching it too much," Rose informed her. The mention of itching her head brought the itchiness to the front of her mind, of course.

"How long was I out this time?" Liliana forced the words out. Her throat was scratchy. She needed a drink. "Can I have some water?" She spotted a jug and a couple of cups on the table to her left. Rose poured her a cup, which she downed in two gulps.

"A couple hours. They said the injury and moving so much to get here caught up with you and your mind went into survival mode. The doctor said you're going to be okay; you just need to rest up and don't bust your stitches. You'll be back to normal in no time." Rose looked less worried now that Liliana was making sense. She felt less confused than before. The couple hours of sleep seemed to have done her some good, plus the painkillers, of course.

"Stitches? Not had those before. Have you heard anything about the fight?" Liliana felt torn between what was going on with her injuries and going into work mode. Reporting on Super fights was her livelihood, after all.

"They arrested the bad guy; Sentinel left him alive. People don't seem to be sure whether that was the right choice, but you know Sentinel doesn't like to take a life unless he must. They haven't released the bad guy's identity yet." Liliana nodded along with Rose. At least she still had the chance to write about the bad guy, whoever he was. "I've heard some people coming up with a name for the bad guy, though. Some are calling him Dark Warrior because he was wearing full-body armour, pitch black. I've got some pictures some citizens got of the fight."

Liliana raised her eyebrow at Rose. She was always in work mode, never switching off.

"I know, I know. But I was stuck in the waiting room for an hour while they looked you over. What else was I going to do?" Rose shrugged her shoulder, waving off the look Liliana was giving her. Liliana chuckled in response.

"So, show me the pictures then." Liliana held out her hand for Rose's phone, which she was palming as she spoke. Rose climbed onto the bed so they could flick through the pictures together.

They weren't of the best quality; the photographer was hiding while snapping the shots. As good as phone cameras were now, fear would always make the camera shaky. There was a dark figure standing across from Sentinel holding a defensive stance. The action sequence shown through the photos showed how they clashed multiple times, both sides taking some hits and going back for more.

Liliana could see where the name Dark Warrior came from. You couldn't see past the armour he was wearing. It was thick but flexible, well designed. In contrast, Sentinel stood tall in a skin-tight suit. His hands, neck and head unprotected. His powers were protection enough, which made Liliana wonder if Dark Warrior had powers or just highly advanced technology. Supervillains normally showed off in battle. This one was different.

Liliana zoomed in on the dark figure in each picture. "Either the person taking these had good timing, or it looks like Dark Warrior stayed defensive throughout the fight. Strange."

"Huh, probably just timing. Why would they stay defensive? Sentinel wouldn't start a fight in the middle of the city for no reason, would he?" Again, Rose appeared blinded by her adoration for the hero.

Before Liliana could disagree, the door quietly

opened. She looked up, expecting to see a nurse coming to check up on her, or maybe Max coming to see how she was doing. Instead, she saw a friendly face, Yates. She wasn't expecting Yates to come. She rarely saw them without Max.

"Ms Masters, I'm glad to see you well," Yates said. They closed the door behind them, checking that no one was about to follow them. They were wearing dark clothing, actively trying to avoid attracting attention. Slim cut trousers blending into the long top and headscarf to match. Only showing the smallest amounts of beige-coloured skin aside from their face.

"Yates, good to see you. Where's Max? Is he okay?" Yates was tense and fidgeting. They paced the room, staring Liliana down.

"You haven't heard?" They were curt, almost on the brink of a nervous breakdown, it seemed.

"Heard what? Yates, where is Max?" Panic rose in Liliana's tight chest. Max had to be okay. She didn't go through a severe concussion and almost suffocate in a subway tunnel only to be told he hadn't made it.

"He's okay. He's alive. But, oh, I don't know how to say this." Yates had switched from pacing to bouncing on the balls of their feet, rubbing their hands together anxiously.

"Just spit it out already." Rose was simply getting annoyed with Yates. They always seemed to get on each other's nerves.

Instead of coming back with a witty retort like they normally would, Yates just turned to the small television caged up in the room's corner ceiling and pressed the power button. The screen flickered to life onto a local news station; they were reporting on the battle between Sentinel and Dark Warrior.

"Sentinel is already helping with the cleanup effort throughout the city, currently working on the rubble pile near the office building on 15th Street, which seemed to take the brunt of the blows between the two fighters."

The feed switched to a shot of Sentinel moving massive blocks of concrete and metal with ease. Liliana thought she saw him flash a smile to the cameras before flipping over great rocks like they were pancakes.

"The brutal fight ended when Sentinel trapped Dark Warrior under an enormous pile of concrete, effectively rendering his weapons useless. After rendering Dark Warrior incapable of fighting, Sentinel unmasked him to the world. Our cameras were nearby and caught the moment for all to see."

The feed switched again to show previously recorded footage. Sentinel tied Dark Warrior up in thick metal cables, making him unable to move his arms to activate any of his technology. Liliana could see him struggling to get free as Sentinel approached and broke the device which was holding his armour together. A strangled cry escaped the face hidden under the dark helmet. Sentinel whipped the helmet off and shattered it on the ground as a flash of dark hair accompanied the face behind the mask.

Liliana felt her breath stop in her throat as she recognised the man everyone knew as Dark Warrior. Blood ran down the man's face from a cut on his forehead, bruises already forming on his soft cheeks. He glared up at Sentinel as he continued to struggle. Sentinel broke more and more pieces of armour off him, exposing the skintight jumpsuit underneath.

"You won't win, Sentinel. Not until you kill me. I will always protect—" Sentinel cut him off by slapping a piece of fabric over his mouth. It stuck to his skin, stopping him from speaking.

Liliana felt tears fall down her face as she stared at the face she'd grown to love. She couldn't understand how this was happening. It was Max. Max was Dark Warrior.

Rose stood up from her hospital bed to get a closer look at the television screen. "What on earth? How is Max Dark Warrior? Did you know?" she asked Yates, who remained silent.

"Yates?" Liliana asked, finding her voice again. She couldn't wrap her mind around this revelation. She knew Max. He wasn't a fan of the Supers, but he didn't hate them. He didn't want them hurt, or anyone. He wouldn't try to hurt anyone. Why would he? It made little sense. Why would he do this?

A memory flashed into her mind from earlier that day. The office building, destroyed. He was fighting Sentinel near her office. If it weren't for her coffee break, she would be dead.

He tried to kill her. No, he wouldn't do that. Would he?

Did she really know him?

"It isn't as it seems, Ms Masters. The media has it wrong. Mr Victor didn't start this fight. Believe me." Yates implored Liliana to listen to them, to believe what they were saying.

"Didn't start the fight? Then who did? Sentinel? Why would Sentinel start a fight that destroyed half the city?" Rose argued. She would always get defensive for Sentinel. Liliana was sure he was the only man Rose ever loved.

"I don't know what happened exactly. But Mr Victor didn't plan for this," Yates shot back at Rose before turning back to Liliana. "You know him, Ms Masters. You know he wouldn't do this."

"Everything I know about Max tells me this can't be true," she admitted reluctantly. "But I can't deny what I'm seeing. Max is Dark Warrior. His fight with Sentinel destroyed my office today. If we hadn't been getting coffee, both Rose and I would be dead right now." Liliana felt her voice rising, feeling the panic of the day's events setting in. "Max lied to me. Plain and simple. He hid this from me. He knew what I would say if he told me. He knew what I would do if I knew he wanted this to happen." Liliana pointed at the television as she shouted. She was angry and confused.

Why would the man she loved do this? She felt conflicted, down to her soul. She loved him, but she feared what he had become. He was a villain in a world where she reported on the heroes. What was she supposed to do with that? What did he think she was going to do now?

"You must believe me. There is more to this than meets the eye. He is not the villain they are making him out to be." Yates held their hands together as if in prayer. As much as Liliana wanted to believe that Max wasn't the villain, she couldn't ignore what she was seeing with her own eyes. She shook her head at Yates. She couldn't believe them over her own eyes.

"Okay. You can't believe me. But please, believe him." Yates pulled an envelope out of their breast pocket and held it out to Liliana.

"Liliana, you can't. You know what Max is now," Rose chimed in, pleading with her to stay on the light side of this argument.

"I know what Max is, that's true, but what I need

to know is why? Why would he do this?" Liliana reasoned, taking the envelope from Yates.

Before they could say anymore, they all heard a commotion down the hall, loud footsteps and, from what Liliana could tell, an angry nurse. Faster than Liliana had ever seen them move, Yates slipped out of the room and moved down the hall in the opposite direction to the commotion, leaving no trace they'd been in the room apart from the noise of the television.

Feeling the heavy weight of Max's letter in her hand, Liliana had the urge to hide it away until she had the chance to read it in private. Stashing the envelope under her hard pillow, she straightened her covers as the door swung open yet again. It would seem the source of the commotion in the hallway was two surly looking police officers.

"Liliana Masters?" the shorter of the two asked. She was round at the hips and wore her brown hair in a tight knot at the nape, a kink in her brow showing her stress level. Given the events of the day, she was most likely run off her feet.

"That's me," Liliana replied, staying polite.

"We have some questions for you regarding Mr Maximus Victor," the taller man stated roughly. He stood at the foot of the bed, almost as broad across the shoulders as the bed was wide. Before Liliana could respond, he turned to Rose who had moved back to Liliana's side. "So, if you could give us some privacy, love?" He nodded his head towards the door.

If there was one thing Rose hated with a passion, it was being patronised, particularly by men who looked down to her.

"Actually, *love,* I think I'll stay. Seeing as my good friend here is currently recovering from a concussion, I think she'd appreciate the support." She stood tall against the man and crossed her arms.

"I don't think you're in a place to speak for Ms Masters—" The man raised his voice, readying himself to shout Rose down, when his partner cut him off.

"She's allowed to stay, Reynolds. If Ms Masters wants her to, of course. This is only an informal interview, anyway."

Reynolds begrudgingly held his tongue, shooting his partner a quick, dirty look. Anyone realised with half a brain he hated his partner. If her gender had something to do with his feelings, Liliana wouldn't be surprised.

"Yes. I would like Rose to stay. I'm still a little fuzzy so I don't know how useful I will be to you, officers," Liliana stated as clearly as she could. She focused on the shorter officer, though she spotted Reynolds roll his eyes over his shoulder. He ignored Rose as if she had done what he told her to do.

"Very well. My name is Detective Nikki Berkowitz. My partner here is Detective Stephen Reynolds. We have some questions about Max Victor and your relationship with him." She was professional and to the point. She flipped open her notebook, ready to take down Liliana's answers.

"I've seen what's been happening on the news. All I can say is that it makes no sense to me. Max wouldn't hurt a soul, not unless someone he knew had been threatened. He doesn't have it in him to be a villain. Not like this." Liliana was adamant that something else was going on here. Max wasn't a villain. "I don't understand how this happened. The Max on the TV isn't the Max I know."

"I'm afraid it is true, Miss Masters. I've seen it for myself. I was present when Mr Victor was brought in." The detective held her gaze firmly. "Mr Victor attacked the city and Sentinel earlier today, causing rather a lot of damage to the city and innumerable injuries. Thankfully, there are not yet any reports of fatalities following the fight. I can only hope that remains the case."

Liliana felt a weight lifted from her shoulders. No fatalities. Regardless of Max's apparent involvement, she was happy to hear no lives were lost in the fight.

"How long have you known Mr Victor?" Detective Berkowitz asked, eyes back on her notepad.

"Almost a year. It's our anniversary in a couple

weeks." Liliana thought that maybe if she helped the detectives she would make them see Max couldn't do what they claimed he had done. That there was more to this story.

"And have you been in a physical relationship the whole time?" Detective Reynolds chimed in.

"I can't see how that's any of your business. But no. We met in my office, became friends and then progressed our relationship a couple of weeks later." Liliana didn't feel comfortable answering detailed questions about her and Max. She just had to remind herself why she was doing this.

"We need to know the details as it gives us a better understanding of your relationship to Mr Victor. It's all part of understanding why he attacked the city," Detective Berkowitz replied. "Although, we do normally ask these questions with a little more tact than that." She shot a quick look over to Detective Reynolds, chastising him silently. He simply grunted in response.

"Did you often spend time at Mr Victor's residence? Or your own?" she continued with the questions.

"It was fifty-fifty, depending on where we needed to be the next day, I suppose. We live across town from each other, so the decision was mainly one of convenience." Though she preferred Max's apartment, she added silently. It was much nicer than her own.

"Do you have a key to his apartment?"

"Yes. And he has one to mine."

"So, you could access his property at your own leisure? Did anything ever stand out to you? Something you didn't expect, given what your own experiences with Mr Victor lead you to believe about his character?"

That felt pointed. They were trying to get her to incriminate Max further.

"No. Nothing like that. No suits of armour. No 'evil' plans to attack the city or Sentinel. Or any of the superheroes."

"He probably kept all of that at a separate property. Keeping his public and private lives apart," Detective Reynolds chimed in again.

"Well, you're not biased at all, are you?" Rose shot across at him.

Detective Reynolds finally looked across at Rose and opened his mouth to shout back at her, but before the words could leave his wide mouth, the door opened yet again.

"Liliana? Liliana!" a voice exclaimed over the heads of all in the room, which had become crowded. A voice which Liliana was very well acquainted with.

"Mother," Liliana replied. Her mother bowled into the room, easily clearing a path through the two detectives. "How are you?"

"How am I? You're in a hospital bed! How are you doing, sweetie?" Liliana's loud mother stood no taller than five foot one but had the presence of a giant, and she let everyone know it.

"I'm fine, Mother, just a mild concussion."

"Good, good. Who are these people?" She finally seemed to notice the two officers she pushed past to get into the room.

"We're detectives, here to interview your daughter regarding her relationship with Mr Max Victor."

"Oh god, don't talk about that man to me. I'm glad you're finally rid of him, Liliana."

Now that confused Liliana. It thrilled her parents to land a man such as Max. His wealth and standing would do well for Liliana and her family. Or so they thought. She could have been miserable, but if she had Max's money they were happy.

"Rid of him? Mother, you love him almost as much as I do!"

"Oh shush. He's a villain, be glad he's locked up." She fluffed Liliana's hard pillow and twitched her sheets, typical fussing.

"You're confusing, Mother." Liliana shook her head and went to speak to Detective Berkowitz again before her mother opened her mouth again.

"You can go now." Her tone had changed as she stared Rose down. Liliana's mother never liked Rose; she didn't agree with her 'lifestyle' as she so elegantly put it. "Her mother is here to look after her. She doesn't need you to stay anymore."

"Mother! Rose is here because she is my best friend. She got me out of the subway tunnel when I passed out and couldn't stand on my own two feet. I would be dead if it weren't for her," Liliana spoke, louder than her mother, the pain throbbing in her head as she raised her voice.

"Nonsense, you need to rest, you don't know what you're saying," her mother replied to her, pushing her down onto the bed fully.

"I'll stay as long as Liliana asks me to. We just had this discussion with the 'lovely' detective over there. I'm staying."

"Yes. What is this about you interviewing my Liliana? Don't you realise she's injured? She's in no fit state to be answering your questions. You need to leave."

Liliana couldn't help but feel embarrassed by her mother. She still treated her like she was twelve and under her control. Liliana felt the blood drain from her thumping head to her cheeks as she blushed from the embarrassment. Her mother shooed the two detectives from the room, not intimidated by their height or their authority.

"Fine. We'll end the interview for now. But we need you to come down to the precinct near your home address once they discharge you to complete the interview." Detective Berkowitz pulled out a card from her faithful notepad and handed it towards Liliana. Of course, her mother snatched it out of the detective's hand to look it over before handing it back to Liliana, who shot a quick glare to the back of her mother's head.

Chapter Six

Liliana's mother pushed her back down onto the bed and tucked in her sheets, fussing over her like she was a child again. She then fussed about the room, silently aside from the occasional tut of disapproval. Liliana watched her fidget across the room, avoiding making eye contact with Liliana.

"Mother?" Liliana asked, trying to get her attention. Instead, she kept moving about the room, fussing with things that didn't really need fussing with. She could tell Rose was getting frustrated with her. She watched her move about the room with a puzzled look on her face.

"Mother!" Liliana half shouted, making her mother jump. She finally made eye contact as Liliana sat back up in the bed, moving the back of the bed into a sitting position with her.

"You should rest, dear." Her mother made a move to get the bed control out of her hand before Liliana pulled it back.

"No. I'm fine. Stop moving around the room so much and talk to me. Is Father okay? Is he here?"

"He's fine. He's back at the shop, keeping it running while I'm here looking after you," she replied, her voice stern. Like it was Liliana's fault for getting a concussion. That woman infuriated her sometimes.

"You don't need to stay if you need to get back. I'm fine, I'll probably be out and home soon enough," Liliana replied, trying to hold back her annoyance from showing.

"I'll be here to watch over her, don't worry," Rose chimed in, placing her hand on Liliana's shoulder. Liliana's mother sucked in a sharp breath at the sight of Rose touching Liliana. She finally looked Rose in the face. Though Rose stood head and shoulders above her, she stood her ground like she was seven feet tall.

"Don't you touch my daughter! I don't want your *illness* catching." She batted Rose's hand away, or rather she tried. Rose wasn't one to back down easily. So, in response, she sat down next to Liliana on the bed and linked arms with her, to which Liliana couldn't help but chuckle a little.

Liliana's mother raised her shoulders tight at the sight. Before she could start a shouting match with Rose, which had happened before, Liliana cut her off.

"I don't want you talking to Rose like that. She isn't ill. She's a normal person who just likes women instead of men." Liliana got her mother's attention and she would not back down this time. She'd had enough of her mother belittling Rose for her sexuality.

"She is ill. That is the only reason to be the way she is," her mother retorted, sticking to her guns.

"You're so small-minded to believe that. Being gay isn't an illness or everyone she meets would 'catch it'," Liliana replied, using air quotes. "YOU would have caught it if that were true!" Liliana pointed out, remembering when she first introduced Rose to her mother. She was a hugger back then.

"Besides," Liliana took a deep breath as she was finally about to tell her mother the truth, "I was bisexual long before I met Rose." That sentence landed with a thud; her mother looked like she'd stopped breathing. Liliana felt Rose tense up beside her. She clearly wasn't expecting her to tell her mother. Not like this, anyway.

Liliana and her mother stared at each other for a moment while the truth sank in. Her mother looked like she was going to say something before she shook her head. She walked out the door as fast as she could, the door slamming shut behind her.

"Well, that went well." Rose's comment filled the room with her sarcasm.

"I never expected to tell her like that," Liliana replied, still staring at the door her mother stormed through. "To be honest, I never expected to tell her, full stop. Not unless I was going to marry a woman."

"I can't believe she would act like that towards you. It's one thing to spout hate to me, but you're her only daughter."

"I believe it," Liliana replied, resigned to having her own mother hate her. "She's never held back before. Why now?"

"That's horrible. She's horrible," Rose retorted, seemingly more upset than Liliana was by this turn of events.

"That's life with the Masters family, I'm afraid. Never happy."

Liliana felt her body sink into the bed, her eyelids heavy with exhaustion. Her mother was tiring to be around even without a concussion. The once hard pillow suddenly felt very inviting. She hoped she would dream of Max once more, her Max, not the image the news was showing. She felt herself slowly relax when the door to her room opened yet again.

"Oh, now what?" Liliana sat up, annoyance shouting through her voice. Almost immediately she regretted her tone and felt her face heat as she saw the doctor walk through the doorway, eyebrows raised at her exclamation.

"Sorry to disturb you, I need to check you over now you're awake." The tall, dark doctor had a smooth, calm voice. He carried a pocketful of pens and devices as he picked up the folder hanging over the edge of Liliana's bed.

"Sorry about that. I'm just exhausted and had a bit of a thing with my mother." She felt the need to be honest with the doctor. Liliana sat up and held her hands in her lap, trying not to look the doctor in the eye. The rush of blood to her face wasn't subsiding, although it no longer felt like embarrassment that held it there. She couldn't help but look at the doctor all over while avoiding his eyes. Liliana heard Rose chuckling under her breath.

Strong hands flipped through her charts and wrote surely illegible notes on various pages. Left-handed, she noticed. That intrigued her. Instead of wearing the typical lab coat most people imagine doctors wearing, her doctor was sporting a crisp shirt tucked into black trousers. Very professional. Liliana felt herself frustrated that the shirt hid what was underneath. She could tell he was well built and kept himself fit, but the shirt gave nothing away to just how fit he was.

The doctor mumbled to himself as he looked through the charts. The noise drew Liliana up to his face. Deep brown eyes, light lips and smooth, dark skin, clean-shaven. Liliana couldn't deny that she fancied him, just a little. She wasn't hiding the fact that she was looking the handsome doctor up and down, and when the doctor met her gaze she realised how obvious she was.

"My name is Dr Richardson; I've been looking after you while you were out. Well, I suppose it was mostly my team of amazing nurses that did the looking after, actually."

"Yes, they've been lovely," Liliana felt herself agreeing with him, smiling all along. She could feel herself about to ruin the moment by giggling when Rose dug her sharp elbow into her ribs to break her attention. "Ow. Oh, Rose, thanks," she mumbled through her embarrassment. She would not live this down, and Rose knew it. If it weren't for the fact they were in a hospital, she would already mock her for her obviousness.

"How are you feeling now you're awake?" Dr Richardson asked her, still flipping through the charts.

"Tired mostly. My head hurts." Liliana rubbed the side of her head, wrapped in bandages again. Her movement brought the doctor's attention to her head as well.

"Yes, you have a rather nasty cut on the side of your head. You needed twenty-three stitches in the end, the bandage is to stop you knocking them in your sleep." He stepped 'round the side of her bed to check the bandage was still in place. It brought him very close, close enough to notice a subtle scent coming off his clothes. It was intoxicating. She breathed it in deep and found herself about to lean in when Rose prodded her again.

"Oh, what's this?" The doctor had noticed the

envelope sticking out from under the rock they claimed was a pillow.

"A letter. I kept it there to read later." Liliana snatched it back from the doctor. She now had Max back in her mind, distracting her from the good doctor.

"Okay." Dr Richardson looked puzzled for a moment; his brow wrinkled in confusion. "Your stitches are taking well. You should only need the bandage for a day or two more. Then you'll be free to go."

"I need to give a statement down at the police station. Am I good to do that tomorrow?" She was looking for the doctor to give her an out.

"As long as you pass our tests in the morning you will be okay," The doctor disappointed her secret wish.

"Okay, so you're doing good for now. I'll be back in a little while to check in again." Dr Richardson smiled at Liliana and Rose before walking out of the room.

"You're so confusing," Rose exclaimed, climbing off the bed. "One minute you're shouting at your mum how you're into women, the next you're mooning over Mr tall, dark and handsome," she chuckled, jabbing fun at Liliana.

"What? Did you not see him? He looks good." Liliana tried not to feel embarrassed.

"Oh yeah, what about Max?" Rose replied, bringing Liliana back to reality.

"Max. What am I going to do about Max?" Liliana brought her knees up to her chest and ran her hands through her hair, over the bandage, her heart torn between what she thought she knew and what it saw today.

She knew Max. At least she thought she did. What was she going to do? Liliana pressed the palms of her hands into her eyes, hoping the pressure would reveal a solution. She loved Max. There was no question about that. Was this how the wives of felons felt? What did they do?

"What would you do, Rose?" Liliana needed advice, perspective on this.

"I don't know. It's an impossible position. You could believe what people are saying, what you're seeing on the news. But we are the news, we know we can get it wrong. What does your heart say? You know Max the best." Rose sat at the foot of her bed, staring into Liliana's eyes.

"Do I though?" Liliana was being pulled in two different directions, her love and her rationality tugging on her just as hard as each other. "My head hurts."

"Yeah, you hit it on a concrete wall." Rose just loved to be sarcastic at the worst times.

"I know that. I have a stress headache and the

stitches. Painkillers won't help this though." The fatigue she felt before Dr Sexy walked in was rushing back to her. "Ugh. I need to sleep."

Liliana relaxed back into her pillow, only to remember the letter she had hidden there, currently tucked underneath the sheets. She pulled it out. It was heavy, hopefully filled with answers. Rose became quiet as she noticed the letter.

"What do you think it says?" she asked in a hushed tone.

"I don't know. I'm afraid to find out. What if it's his confession?" Liliana couldn't take it. The thought of Max being a supervillain brought tears to her eyes. She felt her heart break at the thought.

"I can't stand the tension. You need to open it," Rose determined. She seemed to want to know as much as Liliana did. Liliana nodded, took a deep breath, and slid her thumb under the seal and tugged it open.

Chapter Seven

Thick folded sheets of paper fell out of the heavy envelope, concealing what was written on them. Liliana's hands shook as she picked them up. Something fell out from between the sheets of paper. A photograph. She felt tears drop as she saw herself and Max grinning together. It was from Rose's birthday dinner a couple of weeks before. He'd surprised Rose with reservations at an exclusive restaurant she'd wanted to try for months. It was a double date. Rose's girlfriend at the time was nice, but she thought Max was trying to make a move on Rose. They lasted a little longer after this photograph was taken.

Confusion swirled in her mind, fighting the love that was in her heart, refusing to shift. Liliana turned to the letter, the letter which she hoped would answer all her questions.

Liliana,

My love. I am sorry, sorrier than you can imagine, that it has come to this. This was never my plan.

If Yates has brought this envelope to you, I am most likely being held by the powers that be. I im-

agine I was caught up in a fight with someone, probably Sentinel.

I'm sorry to tell you like this. I am quite the anti-hero, but I am not a bad person. I hope you can still trust me enough to believe me. I never wish harm on anyone, even Sentinel, especially innocent people.

God, I hope no one has been hurt. I hope you are well.

Sentinel is not who the world thinks he is. He is no hero. He is abusing the powers something gifted him with; I'm trying to set right the wrongs he has unleashed in the world.

You're probably wondering why I haven't told you about this before. I suppose it stems from a deep-seated need to keep you safe. I know if you knew about my plans to confront Sentinel, you would want to be involved. He is dangerous; you need to stay away from him. I already know you don't like him. If you knew more, you would go after him as well.

This is something I've been working on for some time before I was lucky enough to run into you on that fateful newsroom floor. I need to see this through.

I suppose if you're reading this I couldn't complete my mission. He is still loose in the city. I need you to believe me.

I love you.

Max

Xxx

Liliana read the letter several times, tears still running down her cheeks. She couldn't believe what Max was saying, but it rang true in her heart.

"What does it say?" Rose asked, a frown on her brow at the tears Liliana was shedding. She wasn't sure what to do. Rose loved Sentinel. She believed in him one hundred percent. What was she going to make of Max's letter?

"He explains everything. He isn't a villain. Though the world won't understand. Not without more proof than this letter offers." Liliana hesitantly passed over the letter. While Rose read it, her brow furrowed more and more, her lips pursed, and her breathing sped up as she read down the letter.

As she finished reading, Rose laid the letter down on the bed carefully while she seemed to consider her thoughts.

"Sentinel, a bad guy? Why does he think that? How can he think that? Look at what he's done for the city, for the world!" Rose tried to stop herself from devolving into a rant. "I know you want to believe him. Hell, even I want to believe him. But Sentinel? He's wrong, he has to be."

"I know, the thought of Sentinel being the man Max says he is is scary. But why would Max lie?

Why would he send me this letter? What good could it do?" Liliana worked through her questions out loud. "What would Max gain by telling me this? What could I do to help him? Nothing! All it would do is it might make me believe he is innocent." Liliana climbed out of bed and paced around the room, trying to ignore her slight dizziness.

"Say I believe him. What next? Am I supposed to go up against Sentinel?" The idea seemed laughable. "Am I supposed to pass this letter on? To the police? Would they even investigate a superhero?" Liliana paused, thinking back to what Max had said at the Mayor's speech earlier. Who will police the Supers?

"That's why he was so upset earlier. He knew Sentinel would be unstoppable." She stopped pacing to stand in front of Rose. It all made sense to her now, and she could see Rose was starting to believe. "He had to take a stand, sooner rather than later. That's why he lost. He wasn't ready."

Liliana could almost see the pieces falling into place. Max wasn't a villain, he was trying to stop the creation of one. Power could go to Sentinel's head if left unsupervised. He would become a villain. He needed to be stopped. Plain and simple.

"What am I supposed to do, Rose?" Liliana could see the completed puzzle, all except her piece. Where did she fit?

"You need to be careful. We don't know who Sentinel is. If he hears you talking like this, you'll be locked up right alongside Max." Rose was afraid. It was clear in her eyes. Rose's breathing picked up. She was panicking.

"Calm down. He isn't here right now. He's busy on the other side of the city. We're safe." Liliana pulled Rose into a tight hug. Not the easiest as she was barefoot and Rose was wearing her favourite heeled boots. Rose panicked for a moment more before Liliana felt her relax into her arms.

"See? We're fine. I'm exhausted and you must be too." Liliana held onto Rose's arms as she calmed down. "Now, do you want to go home and rest?"

"I'd rather not be alone; can I stay here with you? The armchair is surprisingly comfortable."

"Okay then." Liliana glanced out of the small window at the side of her room. The sky was pitch black. "It's late. We should get some sleep, worry about all of this in the morning." She was looking forward to finally getting some rest.

Chapter Eight

The next morning, a surprising amount of sunlight came shining through the small window and onto the shiny floor. Liliana glanced over to the empty armchair and wondered where Rose had got to so early in the day. She didn't have to wonder for long as the door opened to reveal Rose carrying her favourite thing: coffee.

"I love you, Rose," Liliana exclaimed as she reached out for the drink, taking a deep breath in before taking a sip. It was still scalding hot; her room must be near the hospital café.

"Not bad for hospital coffee," Liliana commented approvingly. "You been up long?"

"I couldn't sleep much last night, despite how knackered I was." Rose's eyes betrayed how poorly she slept; dark circles sat underneath tired eyes. "This is actually my second coffee of the morning. Thought you would be awake soon so got you one as well this time. The barista thought me mad, buying three coffees in an hour." She chuckled lightly, blowing on her coffee to cool it quicker.

"What's the latest?" Liliana asked, almost hoping

there was no more news after yesterday.

"He's being moved," Rose stated. Liliana knew she meant Max. "They don't trust him to be safe in the local jail. Too much tech, I suppose. He doesn't have powers, yet they are moving him to the Super jail."

Liliana frowned. "But that's too dangerous for him. The people they hold there? He's not safe there."

"I don't think they're worried about that, Lils. They're more concerned about what he can do rather than what could happen to him."

Liliana felt her heart sink as she pictured what Max was about to experience. She wrote a piece once on the Super jail and the people kept there. They were dangerous beyond comparison. Even if Max was a villain, which she still refused to believe, he didn't belong there. No powers and stripped of tech. He was harmless. The other prisoners would eat him up and spit him out.

She needed to help him. But how?

*

A couple hours later the doctors let her back out into the world, bandage removed and stitches still tender. Rose took a separate cab home to shower and change, which was all Liliana wanted to do right now.

As soon as she stepped into her apartment she noticed some things were different. The police had been here. She felt violated. She didn't want a team of sweaty police officers rooting through her belongings. Could they have done this without telling her? She wasn't sure where the law sat on that issue.

She dropped her keys into the bowl by the front door before putting the chain up, using every lock she had. Not that it would really stop the police, or Sentinel, if they really wanted to get in again. Walking around her living room she noticed cushions out of place, books rearranged, a magazine on the floor which she remembered putting on her coffee table before going to work the day before. One of her kitchen cupboards was partially open. Why would they look at her plates and bowls? At least they didn't leave her fridge open. She didn't need to deal with the smell that would make.

The same in her bathroom. The mirror cabinet was ajar and they mixed her toiletries around. She couldn't believe it; they had moved her toilet roll to be the wrong way 'round. Why?

She almost dreaded looking in her bedroom. What mess could they have made in there? She walked in to see the bed messed up. They had clearly looked under her mattress, a rookie hiding place if she ever saw one. She almost felt insulted. Did they really think she was stupid enough to hide things in such an obvious place?

Further violation, they had looked through her

underwear drawer. She felt the sudden urge to throw it all out and go shopping for new clothes.

Right, first things first, a shower. She stripped down and blasted the shower as hot as she could stand it. She felt all grubby from the previous day's events, so she scrubbed and scrubbed till she felt red raw. She had to be gentle while washing her long hair or else she would damage the stitches.

After a thirty-minute shower, which was very much needed, Liliana set about to get her apartment back in order. Despite scrubbing down the apartment thoroughly, Liliana still felt the intruders. She should feel safe in her home. That comforting feeling had gone. Was moving an overreaction? Maybe, but that was what she wanted to do right now.

Absentmindedly, she switched on her television as she collapsed onto her sofa. She immediately regretted it. Max's face was plastered over all the news channels. Her phone was no welcome distraction, either. She switched it on to see a long list of messages from her parents, all demanding she break off all contact with Max. Like she could have contacted him right now, anyway? Didn't they realise they locked him up?

As she flicked through, ignoring the messages from her parents, she came across some from her friends, all asking if she was okay. As nice as it was to know they were concerned about her wellbeing rather than her relationship status, she could tell they wanted to ask her about Max. Finally, she scrolled down to the end to see a message from Tanya. This was one she dreaded looking at.

Tanya: *Ms Masters, I require your presence at the office ASAP. The news floor is currently closed, therefore, please proceed to the courtyard where we have a makeshift workspace.*

Well, that was abrupt. No word on her injuries, nothing about the building being almost destroyed. Simple instructions. That was Tanya, she supposed.

Why were they still at the office? She got that news never slept, but the building was about to fall last she saw. Surely they wouldn't be back inside the building yet. Liliana had to admit she was curious, so she grabbed her bag and keys before heading out of the apartment that no longer felt like home.

The city around her felt a mix of everyday life and recovery. They left some buildings miraculously untouched, businesses still up and running, lives left intact. Others had been reduced to rubble and stone, injuries uncounted and lives torn apart. Liliana walked through a nightmare, tears falling on one side of the street, the other side trying to figure out what to do. Should they help their neighbours or try to go about life as if everything was fine? She couldn't understand the question.

A café that had got by relatively unscathed was

open, handing out hot drinks and food to people working to rebuild and recover. That was the angle. Liliana believed this is what people should report after such a big fight. Strangers coming together, community strengthening. Liliana jotted some notes down on her phone as she walked past the people helping others. She wanted to take some shots but realised that wouldn't be the right move in this situation.

Running to the bus stop, she hopped onto her ride as it was about to leave, swiping her card before sitting down on the last seat. Letting out a deep breath, she tried to relax as the damaged city rolled past her window.

So much destruction from two people having it out with each other. One of them being her Max. Why didn't he try to take the fight out of the city? The city he loved so much, the city he wanted to protect at any cost. It made little sense to her; she wanted to find him and ask all these questions. Like that was going to happen. The police wouldn't let her anywhere near Max, not if they thought they might have been working together.

All she wanted was to be with Max. To hold him still so she could make sense of everything. To be together again. She could almost feel his hands on her arms, pulling her in close. She allowed herself to close her eyes for a moment as she lent into the memory of Max. Only for a second as the bus came to a stop, rougher than usual, jolting her away from her memory of Max.

"Sorry, folks, seems like we are going to have to reroute here. A piece of building blocks the road ahead. If you need to get off at the next couple of stops, it might be worth walking from here," the bus driver called over the PA system. Liliana saw that her office building was just a couple of streets over, so she stood to get off along with a handful of other passengers.

"You're about to head into the worst hit area," the bus driver called after the little group that had disembarked. "Be careful where you go, some bits aren't stable yet, apparently."

The small group looked around warily before splitting up, continuously looking up for falling debris. Liliana saw there were one or two areas blocked off from the public. They must be the unstable areas. She noted to avoid them if possible.

Continuous detours around fallen concrete and burst pipes made the short walk longer. She felt like she was walking through a maze to get to her office, still unsure of what she was going to find when she got there. If it weren't for the message from Tanya, she would have thought they had moved to another office building. Though, she wasn't sure of where they would have gone.

Rounding the last corner, she saw the state of the building. How Tanya had gained access, she did not know. It looked ready to collapse. Liliana really didn't want to step foot in the office.

Liliana's heart skipped a beat as a hand reached out and grabbed her elbow, pulling her back towards the neighbouring building. She turned her head to see a familiar face. One of the office interns pulled her towards a marquee she hadn't spotted. The marquee was being used by the office staff. At the centre of the hustle and bustle stood Tanya, barking orders out to everyone around her.

Tanya set them up right next to Carl's café, right where she and Rose were when the fight reached them. Right where Rose saved her from being squashed by a flying car door. Liliana pushed through the madness surrounding Tanya and grabbed her attention away from yelling at people.

"Tanya!" Liliana shouted over the din surrounding them. Tanya looked over and clocked who was standing right in front of her.

"Ah, Ms Masters. Follow me." She turned and walked through the crowd, which parted like the Red Sea to let her through. Liliana hurried after her, following her into Carl's café where she had set up a makeshift office. "Take a seat."

Sitting across from each other in one of Carl's well-worn booths, Tanya pulled out a recorder and notebook.

"What are those for?" As far as Liliana knew, this was just meant to be a brief chat.

"Ms Masters. I understand the fight caused you injuries?" Tanya had switched into interviewer mode. Maybe she was collecting everyone's view of the fight for a story?

"Yes. I was in the subway tunnel with Rose and hit my head on the concrete wall. Rose got me to the hospital yesterday and they checked me over," she replied.

"And they let you go?" Tanya asked.

"Obviously."

"You didn't check yourself out? Not in a hurry to get out at all?" Tanya probed.

"No. Why would I be in a hurry to leave the hospital? I passed out twice and had a load of stitches in my head. I couldn't walk straight for a bit."

Tanya nodded and squinted her eyes a little. This was feeling like an interrogation rather than a chat or interview.

"Not in a hurry to see Mr Victor?" There it was. Liliana frowned and remained silent. Tanya wanted the dirt on Max. She didn't care that Liliana had been unaware of what happened, who everyone thought Max was.

"Were you aware of who the man really was?" Tanya asked, trying to dig deeper.

"I... No. There's more to him than this, I'm sure of it," Liliana stumbled over her words, not sure of what to say. What was going to be reported from this?

"Mr Victor dealt a lot of damage to the city, a lot of injuries. Particularly to this company. My building seemed to be targeted. Did you piss Mr Victor off? Did you have an affair? Why would he target you like this?" Tanya reeled off the questions before Liliana had a moment to process them.

"What do you have to say to the man who saved you: Sentinel?" she finished, waiting for Liliana's response.

"No, I didn't cheat on Max. He wasn't targeting me. He has no reason to want me dead. There's more to this. There has to be," Liliana replied, her face getting hotter as she got angrier.

"So, you are standing by Mr Victor?" Tanya replied, her eyebrows raised in surprise.

"No. Wait. I don't condone what happened yesterday. All I'm saying is that there is more to what happened than meets the eye," Liliana tried to clarify, leaning into the recorder to make sure it got her words correctly. "Why are you asking me all these questions?"

Tanya ignored Liliana's question and carried on with her own interrogation.

"Does it not matter to you your boyfriend hurt people yesterday? He killed people." That made her stop. She didn't think anyone died during the fight. That's what the police officers told her.

"Wait. People died? Who?" she asked, tears forming in her eyes. Max couldn't have done this. He couldn't have killed people. That wasn't him.

"Yes. Many of them our own people. People you worked with every day. Your boyfriend killed my staff," Tanya replied, somehow staying emotionless.

"Who? Tanya, tell me who!" Liliana raised her voice for the first time against Tanya. How was she staying so calm about this, talking about people she employed being killed? Any normal person would be distraught by this.

"That intern, the one who started yesterday. I believe you knew him."

No. Not Johnathon. He had just started, he was so young. Liliana slumped back into the booth as Tanya reeled off some more names, people she had worked with, some more than others. But Johnathon stuck in her mind. He had been in the coffee shop with her and Rose. If he hadn't rushed back, he would be here, being ordered about by Tanya.

"The fact of the matter here is that your boyfriend is a murderer. He'll never see the light of day again. I understand the police have him firmly locked away. I'm not entirely convinced you should walk free either. You were so lovey-dovey about each other, you must have known about him." Tanya dug her claws into Liliana's heart as she drove home her message.

"I didn't know. How many times can I say it? I'm just as surprised by his involvement in all of this as everyone else. More so, actually. I thought I knew him," Liliana tailed off, tears falling down her face as she pictured Johnathon in her mind.

"You may have convinced the authorities of that, but not me, Ms Masters. I think it's best you don't come back to my company again." That brought Liliana out of her mind and back into the booth with Tanya.

"Wait. You're firing me?" she asked. She couldn't believe Tanya. She brought her in to interrogate and fire her. After everything that she had done for the company? She had poured her blood, sweat and tears into this job. For what?

"I'm afraid we cannot have someone with your background on this team," Tanya replied, cool as ever.

"Don't bother. I quit. You're a horrible bitch of a woman." Liliana couldn't stop herself from telling Tanya what she really thought of her, before storming out of the café and back through the marquee, barely having time to savour the look on Tanya's face at her insult.

She pushed past several people who stayed behind her at Tanya coming out of the café with a sour look on her face.

"Don't bother coming back for your things, your boyfriend destroyed them when he attacked my building," Tanya called after Liliana.

More people turned to stare at Liliana as she stormed off and hailed a cab at the nearest open road. Before she knew what she was doing, she had given the driver Max's address. Not his house up on the hilltop above the city. He kept an apartment in the city for when he had to stay late at work. Liliana wasn't sure if she was going to get in, though. The police might have blocked it off.

She just wanted to feel near to Max. Despite everything, she knew Max wasn't a killer. Did that make her a bad person? To trust Max over what had happened to Johnathon? She felt split down to her core. If Max was a villain, what did that make her? She held her head in the palm of her hands as she tried to figure out what was going on.

A few minutes later, the cab pulled up outside of Max's apartment building. The driver was thankfully quiet and didn't know about the connection she had to Max. She really needed that right now. Stepping out of the cab and walking towards the building, her phone beeped at her.

Rose: *I heard what happened with the devil witch. Are you ok?*

Liliana: *I'm pissed off. Need some time to clear my head. I'm at Max's.*

Rose: *What on earth are you doing there? Aren't the police crawling all over his house?*

Liliana: *No one's here for now. Think I'm allowed in. I'll call you once I calm down and sort my head out.*

She loved Rose, but she needed some peace and quiet to work things through. Despite everything, she felt safe here. Max's apartment was empty. It didn't look like the police had searched through it yet. Hopefully they would leave it alone, leave her alone. Alone with Max.

Chapter Nine

Liliana sank into the deep couch in Max's living room, surrounded by blankets they shared. She felt closer to home than in her own apartment. She could smell Max's cologne on the cushions. It brought back many happy memories, going back to the start of their relationship. Max brought her here after their third date.

*

"You have two homes? Why aren't I more surprised?" Liliana exclaimed, taking in the apartment for the first time.

"I have two homes in the city. This penthouse and an actual house on the hilltop looking over the city," Max replied, smiling at Liliana's amazement.

"Why did you say 'in the city' specifically? Let me guess, holiday homes." Liliana shook her head as she was once again reminded of Max's immense wealth.

"I have a log cabin in Canada, a beach house in the Canaries and a small island off the coast of Japan," Max reeled off his list of homes. *"But I rent out several of them to holiday makers when I know they are going*

to be empty. The proceeds go towards my charitable foundations."

"Ah, so you don't sound as big-headed as people might think hearing that list," Liliana chuckled. She knew he wasn't like that anyway, but it was enjoyable to poke fun.

"Exactly," Max replied, heading through an open door to what Liliana thought to be the kitchen. She followed and saw a bright room filled with wooden cabinets. Max opened a cabinet, floor-to-ceiling length, revealing several dozen bottles of wine. The cabinet was half refrigeration, half storage, splitting the white from the red. Max turned to Liliana to ask for her preference.

"White, please. Dry," she answered his unasked question. He pulled a bottle out from the middle of the fridge and collected a couple of glasses before leading Liliana over to the couch in the spacious living room.

Liliana relaxed into the soft cushions as Max handed her a glass of chilled wine.

"So, I've not scared you off yet?" Max asked, unsure of the answer.

"No. Not yet," Liliana smiled as Max moved a little closer. "Although this is a little intimidating. My apartment has to be a quarter of the size of this place." Liliana looked around as Max chuckled at her answer.

"I'm sure your home is as lovely as you are." Max's

deep voice drew Liliana in further, the wine almost forgotten.

"You haven't seen it yet. This place is amazing and I'm sure I haven't seen half of it," Liliana rambled on as Max inched closer and closer. She couldn't help it. She was being drawn into his bright-green eyes. Like a calm meadow, they're beautiful.

Liliana felt the warmth of Max's breath as he pulled her closer to him, powerful hands on her waist, moving up to gently cup her face as he finally closed the gap between them. Lips touched, and Liliana felt the air leave her body. She fell into his body completely as the kiss took over her mind. Max was soft and strong in all the right places as he drew the kiss out as long as it could go before they had to stop for air.

"Wow," they both exclaimed together as their lips finally parted, leaving them slightly panting. Liliana only remembered the glass of wine she was holding as it spilled onto Max's expensive-looking blue rug.

"Oh shit! I'm so sorry!" Liliana jumped up from the couch, leaving Max to fall against the cushions she was just using. Liliana looked around for something to mop up the wine as Max realised what had happened.

"Oh, don't worry, I'll grab something." Max went through another door and came back with a spray bottle and some cloths. Before Liliana could move to take them to clear up her mess, Max dropped to the floor and mopped up the spilled wine. "There we go.

Good as new."

Max put down the cleaning supplies and took what remained of Liliana's wine from her and placed it next to his full glass. He stepped over the wet patch on the rug and pulled Liliana in close for another kiss.

*

She and Max shared many memories in this apartment. She had hoped to make some more. She did not know what was going to happen now. Was she even allowed to be here? Max had given her a key a couple of weeks ago, but was this even Max's anymore? Had the police seized it? She had no clue. But she was going to stay here for as long as possible.

A couple of hours later, the doorbell rang. Her food had arrived; she didn't have the energy for cooking. Buzzing the delivery guy up, she dug out the fancy chopsticks Max kept in his kitchen. He had an amazing Chinese takeout place right around the corner from here. It was their favourite place to order from on a late-night date.

She opened the door at the right time to stop the delivery guy from knocking. She thanked him and handed over the money, plus a generous tip. It must not be fun being back at work so soon after the attack. He probably needed the money to be working tonight. Not two seconds after closing the door, there was a knock. Had she got the money wrong? She opened the door to see someone completely different.

"Yates? What are you doing here?" Liliana could swear the hallway was empty a moment ago, apart from the delivery guy. She stood aside to let them into the apartment.

"I could ask you the same thing, Ms Masters," Yates replied, scanning the room quickly before turning to face Liliana.

"Liliana, please. It's one thing when you're actively working for Max, it's just weird when it's just the two of us."

"I am still working for Mr Victor, Ms Masters." Yates watched Liliana closely, gauging her reaction.

"He's in prison. You can't be working for him," Liliana stated, now sure that something else was going on.

"My employment contract exceeds imprisonment," Yates replied.

"Well, that's vague as anything," Liliana responded. "Come sit down with me. I've ordered enough food for four, help yourself."

Yates seemed unsure about relaxing their high standards in front of Liliana. "Okay. I have some important things to discuss with you." They walked to the dining table with Liliana, who grabbed another set of chopsticks from the kitchen on the way.

Together they spread out the food between them

and ate in an awkward silence, each waiting for the other to speak first.

"Ms Masters, I hope you don't mind me saying, but I believe you know there is more going on than it seems with Mr Victor." Yates seemed uncomfortable sitting across from Liliana. They were usually standing in a more professional setting.

"It doesn't all add up, if that's what you mean."

"Yes, Mr Victor engaged Sentinel in combat, but it wasn't in order to destroy the city. Mr Victor believed Sentinel had ulterior motives with the new superpowered Taskforce the Mayor announced. Mr Victor was trying to stop Sentinel before he could do any damage. But his plans fell through." Yates ate a few bites of food before continuing. "Something occurred between Mr Victor and Sentinel just before the fight began. I saw they had an intense, but short, conversation. I believe Mr Victor tried to talk Sentinel down before resorting to combat. Sentinel must have said something to anger Mr Victor."

Yates somehow relaxed as they spoke. They had this entire speech building up since the fight, unable to discuss it with anyone other than Liliana. She had never known Yates to speak so much in one conversation; they were usually a person of few words. This was a new side to them.

"What do you think Sentinel said to Max? It must have been something big if Max resorted to violence. That isn't like him." Liliana wished she had the answers. She needed to speak to Max more than anything else. Hear his side of the conversation.

"I don't know, Ms Masters. I should have built a recorder in Mr Victor's suit; we could have the proof we need to get him out of that prison if I had." Yates was obviously blaming themselves for this.

"You couldn't have known something like this was going to happen, don't blame yourself." Liliana reached across the table to take Yates's hand in comfort. "Wait a minute. You built the suit?" Her eyebrows hiked up into her hairline. She did not know Yates had the skills to build something like that.

"Yes, I did. Mr Victor had some requests for the suit, and I carried them out as much as possible." Yates said it like it was nothing. Humble to a fault.

"That's incredible. I saw the suit on the news, and a little in person, I'm impressed." Yates let a small smile through at the compliment.

"Thank you, Ms Masters, you're kind to say that," they replied, avoiding eye contact as they continued eating.

"So, what are we going to do about this? How can we get Max out?" Liliana asked, sure now more than ever that Max didn't deserve to be locked up for the fight. "Did he keep any proof of what Sentinel was up to?"

"He kept some papers and some notes in the workshop. There might be something there we can use," Yates replied, considering the options.

"Workshop? What workshop?" Liliana replied. She had been to his house, and all over this apartment, but had seen no sign of a workshop.

"He hadn't around to showing you the workshop yet. Mr Victor was unsure of telling you about it and his suspicions on the superheroes," Yates replied, shoulders hunched in uncertainty again. "It's underneath the Hilltop property, not shown on building plans so the authorities shouldn't be aware of it."

"Okay, I'm going to ignore Max's mistrust of me for now, that's going to be a long conversation for a later date. Can we get into the workshop without the police knowing? They must have eyes on his house by now." Liliana felt a plan forming, finally something for her to do. She was going to get Max out of prison somehow. She was going to talk to him again and get him to tell her the truth this time. No more secrets.

Chapter Ten

After Liliana and Yates finished their dinner, they scouted out the workshop together, using the darkness as a cover should the police be nearby, monitoring the house as well. Yates drove them to the hillside, but they didn't take the main road as Liliana expected.

"I thought we were heading to Hilltop?" Liliana asked, looking back at the turn she expected them to take.

"We are. Mr Victor keeps a separate entrance for the workshop. It's come in useful for this occasion," Yates replied, pressing a button on the wheel of the car. Liliana looked around them to see a small light on their right. The button Yates pressed had opened a small gap in the hillside, which got bigger as they approached. It was just big enough to let the vehicle into a dimly lit tunnel. The car's headlights lit the path ahead as they sped through the tunnel.

Liliana wouldn't have had the guts to drive so fast down a dark tunnel. Yates must have driven down here often enough to know where they were going so well. After a minute or two of not being able to see very far in front of them, a bright light appeared at the end of the tunnel. It sped towards them, briefly blinding Liliana.

Blinking furiously as her eyes watered from the sudden explosion of light, Liliana saw a vast car park around them. Yates reversed into a space, the tunnel straight ahead of them. Liliana clambered out of the car to look at the variety of vehicles around them. Her eyes were then drawn above them to see large windows into what must have been the workshop. Her jaw dropped as she took in the size of the operation Max was hiding beneath his house.

"This is some next-level, Batman shit here," she exclaimed before she could stop herself. "How did Max hide all of this under here? It's insane!"

"I remember Mr Victor saying something along the same lines when he discovered this cavern," Yates laughed slightly as they watched Liliana's reaction. "We worked together to build the workshop several years ago when the superheroes became more entrenched in the city. He wanted to be prepared in case things went sideways."

"You've been together for a long time, haven't you?" Liliana asked. She didn't know too much about Yates, aside from their employment with Max.

"Nearly twelve years now. Since Mr Victor got

into trouble in my homeland. He accidentally insulted a local leader while on holiday. I talked the leader down, thankfully. After that, Mr Victor asked me to come work for him, making sure he doesn't get into that situation again." Yates looked back on their history fondly, their loyalty showing through.

"Thank you for helping him. I know we haven't known each other for very long, but I am grateful for all you do to keep him safe. I would never have met him without you looking out for him."

"It's not always been easy. He does like to get himself into trouble without an escape plan in mind," Yates chuckled, remembering their adventures with Max.

"So, what else do you have hidden away here?" Liliana was keen to explore the workshop. If Max's suit was any sign, there must be loads of cool tech hidden here.

Yates led Liliana over to a doorway, a staircase leading up into the galley above the parking lot.

"There's a fair bit of tech here. Failed experiments and theoretical designs. Mr Victor often took inspiration from the Supers, trying to replicate their abilities. He thought that if it came down to a fight between himself and a rogue Super, using their own abilities against them was the only way to stand a chance," Yates explained. It made sense, but it sounded complicated. How could you replicate a Super's powers? No one really understood how they came to be.

"Was he focusing on any Supers, aside from Sentinel?" Liliana asked.

"He was focusing on the more local Supers to start with. Sentinel has flight, strength, invulnerability. The big three, I suppose." Yates walked over to an enormous desk covered with papers and tools. "Lightbringer has control over fire, so Mr Victor believed something controlling fire suppressants might work. It would have to be an intense form of suppression to combat the temperatures Lightbringer can create."

"I don't know how a woman who can create fires with her mind became a superhero. Sounds far too dangerous a power to be used. And how is it helpful in most situations?" Lightbringer always confused Liliana.

"For Glassier, Mr Victor designed a ball that will emit a wide spectrum of light, designed to counteract their invisibility powers. It acts fast enough that Glassier can't work around it straight away. It has a limited effect, but useful if you need to move fast against them."

Liliana nodded along with Yates's explanation of Max's work. How he got all this work done without her noticing, she did not know.

"If Max was working on all of this in secret, how much time did he actually spend at the office?"

"Mr Victor has had several VPs taking over some of his responsibilities lately. Allowing him to take a step back from the day-to-day tasks and simply overseeing the company from afar."

"More lies," Liliana frowned, again questioning why she was doing this. Why did she still feel loyal to a man who lied to her from the moment they met? What was she going to do when she saw him again? At the moment, she felt torn between a kiss and a punch. Maybe both.

Liliana walked around the enormous desk, looking over the tech designs Max had been working on while she pondered their future, together or apart, when she noticed a small drawer on the side of the desk. She pulled it open, expecting to see some more design tools or smaller papers. Instead, a small box slide to the front of the drawer. Liliana picked it up and opened it to see a bright diamond set in a simple silver band. The air quickly left her chest as she saw the engagement ring sitting in the box in her hand.

"He was going to propose?" Liliana asked quietly. "Did you know anything about this Yates?" She turned to see a surprised look on Yates's normally stoic face. "I'm guessing not."

"No. Mr Victor had mentioned nothing about a ring to me. It must have been recent though; I had only collected some items from that drawer last week," Yates replied.

"Last week. He was going to propose. I wonder if he was going to ask at dinner the other night." Liliana was getting caught up in her imagination, her love for Max flaring in her chest as she pictured the moment, saying yes, planning a wedding with her Max. Her imagination took her all the way to saying their vows before reality came rushing back.

"He was going to propose without telling me the truth about what he was doing." She had circled back around to anger. She was furious with Max. Furious that he didn't think he could trust her with this. He knew they shared the same views of the Supers and how reliant the city was on them. Why didn't he think she would share the same views on what needed to be done?

Alright, so she may have tried to stop him from confronting Sentinel head-on. That was an idiotic idea. But they could have worked together on an actual solution.

"How could he do this to me?" Liliana asked. Yates looked unsure if they should answer. This was not the reaction they expected from a ring discovery.

"I need to speak to Max," she decided.

"How are you going to do that? Mr Victor is being kept away from visitors," Yates asked.

"We're going to break him out, that's how."

Chapter Eleven

"Right, people, we have less than an hour to get the final edits over to the printers for the morning paper. Get me your work in ten minutes or don't come back," Tanya, the hell-bitch-come-editor-in-chief, shouted over the heads of her minions under the marquee outside of Carl's café. Rose, practically attached to her laptop, attempting to make some last-minute touches to some photographs for the many articles the surrounding journalists were working on. The pace had picked up since Liliana had left or been fired. No one was sure what had happened. She also wasn't responding to Rose's texts, and she was getting worried.

She hoped Liliana was just sleeping off the week's events, but she still worried. She shot off a quick text again before finishing her photos.

"Ms Wilson. Are you done yet?" Tanya barked over the pool of interns surrounding her.

"Just finished now and uploaded to the server," Rose shouted back.

"Good. I have several other photographers in the field today, so I don't need you until the morning," Tanya dismissed Rose with an icy wave of her hand.

Why did she work here? For her? Rose asked herself, taking a deep breath, stopping herself from telling Tanya what she really thought of her. Instead, she packed up her laptop and camera, telling herself that one day it'll be the last time she put up with Tanya's crap attitude. Rose didn't even really pay attention to where she was walking until she almost fell over one barricade surrounding her half-destroyed office.

"Whoa there, ma'am. Careful where you step," a familiar voice broke through Rose's annoyance, in time for her to fall into the voice owner's arms. Her breath caught in her throat for multiple reasons. The main one being the owner of the arms wrapped around her waist, stopping her from falling flat on her face and destroying the tech in her arms.

"Sentinel," Rose stated, shocked to run into him for the second time in several months. Most people never run into a superhero unless they were in danger or were a villain themselves.

After a beat, Rose realised Sentinel's arms were still on her waist, sucking in her breath as she jumped back from Sentinel. How was she meant to act around him? After hearing what Max had written to Liliana, she did not know if Sentinel could be trusted anymore. Was he even a hero?

"Thank you. I wasn't looking where I was going." Rose tried to remain neutral. Movement in the corner of her eye drew her attention away from Sentinel, who was simply staring straight into her eyes. If she were the type to be attracted to men, she would blush and stumble over her words under his gaze. The movement turned out to be cameras. Sentinel was being filmed helping the city repair the buildings affected by his fight with Max.

"I recognise you. Aren't you a friend of Liliana Masters? The girlfriend of Dark Warrior?" Sentinel asked, although he sounded like he already knew the answer.

"Yes," Rose replied hesitantly. She did not know how Liliana wanted to handle the press. It was odd being on this side of the news. She was normally the one behind the camera. She could tell that the cameraman was very interested in her conversation with Sentinel. Shots of him interacting with 'normal' people must be worth her weight in gold.

"Do you know where she is? I would very much like to speak to her about Max," Sentinel asked.

"I don't, actually. I've been trying to get ahold of her. She got hurt in the fight, so I imagine she's resting up," Rose replied.

"Ah, I didn't know she was hurt. Is she doing okay?" Sentinel asked. It almost sounded convincing that he cared, but something about him shouted fake.

"She'll be okay," Rose replied, not wanting to give out any specifics, especially on camera.

"Excellent. Well, if you speak to her, could you let her know I would like to speak to her? She can contact me here." Sentinel pulled a card out from his suit somewhere and handed it over. Rose had never known a superhero to hand out contact details before. He must really want to see Liliana.

"Of course," Rose replied, surprised. "If you could excuse me, I need to get going." She backed off before he could ask any more questions.

"Ah yes, sorry for keeping you. Just be sure to watch out for any more stumbling blocks from here on," Sentinel waved her off with a fake-looking smile on his face. He turned back to the camera, a smile shining across his face.

Rose walked off, feeling a lot more uncomfortable than the last time she met Sentinel. It was like she had just been wearing rose-tined glasses the last time. Now she could see the act he was putting on for the public, she could see he wasn't the nice guy the city made him out to be. There was something unsettling going on under his skintight suit.

*

Moonlight shone down on the prison complex spread out across a half mile of land below the hill. Liliana perched low on the grass, binoculars in hand. Twelve-foot-tall fences surrounded the prison, with watchtowers at regular intervals.

Seemingly impenetrable. Her resolve to get Max out admittedly faltered slightly before she pushed the doubt out of her mind.

This was about more than her love for Max. She needed answers, she needed to speak to Max. If she didn't like the answers he gave, she could always leave him in the prison. Breaking in was the chief thing she needed to do.

Looking away from the prison for a moment, she noted down what she had seen. She and Yates had been scoping out the prison for a couple of hours now, realising how big a task they had set for themselves.

Yates was easy to get on board with the prison break idea. They had down to the planning quickly after they decided. They both agreed that Liliana needed to avoid talking about Max in public to keep the attention away from what they were doing. If she started shouting about the truth about Sentinel and Max, then the police would suspect they would try a prison break. It hurt, but Liliana would have to speak out against Max to save their cover.

"Shift change, 01:30 am. Seems to be a thirty-minute handover period," Yates stated as Liliana noted it down. Yates appeared to have switched to military mode as soon as they began planning the prison break, which only raised more questions about their background. Questions Liliana didn't feel comfortable asking just yet.

"How long do you think we should do recon for? This is all very new to me," Liliana asked quietly, not taking her eyes off the prison.

"A week or two, I should think. Enough time to understand shift patterns. Prisons have to be strict with their operation so we shouldn't see any deviation from the pattern," Yates replied. Now they explained, it all made sense to Liliana. Now she felt the heat in her cheeks, embarrassed she felt she had to ask the question.

Liliana felt like she was in a spy novel, trying to stay under the radar by day, scouting out a prison by night. It still didn't feel very real to her. Her boyfriend was trapped somewhere in the building they were watching, going through extreme interrogation, possibly by Sentinel himself. They had yet to spot Sentinel arriving or leaving the prison, but they expected him to visit Max at some point. In the past Sentinel had made a point of seeing his enemies behind bars. Liliana thought he did it to make sure they were being kept safely behind bars. Not anymore. Now Liliana saw his motivations for what they really were, a publicity stunt. He wanted to spend as much time in front of the camera as possible.

Sentinel must have been loving the exposure he was getting after his battle with Max. The cameras had barely left him alone ever since Max was arrested. Liliana watched the news, seeing what Sentinel was up to most days, but she hated the love and adoration Sentinel was getting. It was all so unfair to Max. They weren't even trying to understand why Max would apparently become a supervillain, no attempt to discover the truth of things. Just throw him in prison and praise Sentinel. It was all so twisted.

"Heads up." Yates pulled Liliana out of her internal monologue to see a large vehicle pulling up to the prison gates. Liliana looked closer at the vehicle and saw a heavily armoured truck, big enough to fit an entire team of soldiers. The markings on the side of the truck labelled it as the National Guard, though why they would arrive at the prison, Liliana couldn't tell. After a brief pause, it granted the truck access and pulled through to the underground parking lot. As far as they could tell, the bulk of the visitors parked underneath the administration building and disappeared inside until they left.

"There must be an internal system letting them into the building and into the prison itself. We might stand a chance of sneaking in through the parking area if we have the right passes. I'll look into it tomorrow," Yates theorised, while Liliana noted down the truck in her notebook.

The rest of the night passed with little more activity, another shift change at 9 am and the truck left not an hour after it arrived. The reason for its visits still a mystery to the spies on the hill.

Chapter Twelve

"Ms Masters, thank you for coming down," Detective Berkowitz said, walking through a set of double doors to see Liliana standing in the police's reception.

Liliana had to face the fact that she was about to be questioned again about Max. This time she didn't have a raging headache to contend with, thankfully. Though she also didn't have Rose by her side. She felt lonely without her best friend to lean on. The reception of the station was a dim grey colour. Several aging posters covered the walls, encouraging people to 'do the right thing' and to 'say no to illegal drugs', the typical sort of thing.

The receptionist behind the plexiglass seemed dull to the world. He had probably seen too many types of people pass through the station to be interested anymore. He had barely looked up from filing his nails to register Liliana's presence. He had half-heartedly typed a few things into his computer before directing Liliana to the seating area. She hadn't been able to sit down. The waiting area was far too busy, and she was honestly thankful because the seats looked like they were never washed.

Detective Berkowitz led Liliana back through the double doors, deeper into the station. Liliana took a deep breath as she felt like she was diving into the belly of the beast.

"We are just in here." Berkowitz led Liliana into a small room, a table and chairs in the middle, with a small kitchenette to the side.

"Not the interrogation room?" Liliana blurted out before she could stop herself.

"This is just an interview, not an interrogation. Unless there's a reason to treat it as an interrogation?" Detective Berkowitz replied, raising her thin eyebrow at Liliana.

"No. No reason, I was just expecting the full-on interrogation room you see on TV is all," Liliana replied, trying to calm her racing heart.

"You shouldn't believe everything you see on TV, Ms Masters," Berkowitz replied with a smirk.

"Don't I know it," Liliana said under her breath. She sat down at the table as Berkowitz brought over a couple of coffees.

"Sugar?"

"No, thank you," Liliana replied, taking the cup from Berkowitz.

"So, I just have a couple of questions today about

your relationship with Max Victor," Berkowitz started as soon as she sat down. She pulled out a notebook from her inside pocket, opening it on a well-worn spine. Liliana took a deep breath as she prepared for the questions.

"When did you first meet Mr Victor?" Okay, starting off with a simple question.

"A little over a year ago," Liliana replied.

"How did you meet?"

"I ran into him, literally, in the hallway of my office building. He was doing an interview for the paper and my colleague Rose had just taken some photographs for the feature," she replied, thinking back to that fateful day.

"You ran into him?"

"Yeah. I wasn't looking where I was going, and he was walking out of a room just at the wrong moment for us to collide. He caught me before I could hit the floor face first." Liliana couldn't help a small chuckle escape as she remembered the day.

"And you began dating shortly after? Is that right?"

"Yes, he took me out to dinner a couple days after we met."

"I see, and you had a good relationship?" Getting a bit more personal now, Liliana felt uncomfortable with the questions.

"Yes. We were happy," Liliana replied. Then she remembered she needed to deny that she knew anything about Max's secret identity to the police. "Although, I obviously didn't know everything about him at this point. Only what he showed me." Berkowitz nodded along to what she was saying.

"Of course," she said, noting everything down in her notebook. "And where did you spend most of your time together? When you weren't out and about in the city." Odd question.

"We would normally be up at Hilltop or in my flat. A couple of months ago he purchased an apartment in the city for us to both use rather than have me trekking up to Hilltop whenever I spent the night. We were using it as a trial for moving in together."

"An apartment?" Berkowitz flicked pages back and forth, her brow furrowed. "I have no record of an apartment in the city under Mr Victor's name."

"Like I said, it was a recent purchase. How old is your information?" Liliana enquired, curious why the apartment wouldn't have shown up.

"What's the address?" Berkowitz asked, ignoring Liliana's question in favour of her own. Liliana supplied the address, which Berkowitz jotted down quickly. "One moment, I just need to pop out. I'll be right back." Berkowitz left the room before Liliana could reply.

Should she have mentioned the apartment? If they

didn't know about it, maybe Max wanted to keep it hidden from the authorities? Liliana's feet started twitching, her heart thudding in her ears. The seconds ticked by without Berkowitz returning as her anxiety rising. She felt that pressure in the back of her throat, meaning she was reaching the verge of an anxiety attack.

Ticking rang across the room as the clock on the wall seemed to get louder every time it announced that time was slipping away from Liliana. After what seemed like an age, the doorhandle creaked open once more, Berkowitz came back in, unaware of how her actions had almost sent Liliana spiralling. She struggled to take several deep breaths, bringing her heart rate back under control as Berkowitz resettled herself at the table and sat opposite Liliana.

"So, a search of the address you gave me has shown that the apartment in question is under the ownership of a certain Yates Ayad. We could not track this Yates down; however, we have a record of a note allowing Mr Victor and yourself to remain at the property until further notice. A strange situation we haven't seen before." Berkowitz stared at Liliana, waiting for information she didn't have.

Max must have known she might need the apartment as a refuge. He must have known they could capture him. He kept the apartment as a safe house the authorities couldn't seize, somewhere for Liliana to retreat if needed. It was smart keeping it under Yates's name; they weren't in the investigation's eye. Though, Liliana couldn't figure out why. If she were investigating a rich supervillain, the first person she would question would be the person who spent the most amount of time with him. And that was Yates, plain and simple.

"Odd. I thought Max owned it himself," Liliana replied, offering no information on Yates. She felt like she was in the middle of a secret and she did not know her role in it, just deciding as and when needed, hoping she was heading in the right direction.

"Yes. Strange." Berkowitz lingered, looking Liliana straight in the eye, waiting for her to falter. After a moment or two, she slowly turned back to her trusty notebook. "Were there any times when you suspected Mr Victor was hiding anything from you?"

"Not that I recall. I trusted him." Liliana remembered she needed to be against Max publicly. This interview was public enough to warrant some acting on her part. "Of course, I feel silly now, not seeing it. I can't trust him, not if he were planning something like this." The words felt heavy in her mouth, the lie jumping out far too easily. She never expected to be in this situation, telling lies to the police to protect herself and her boyfriend. It was wrong, but it needed to be done. Otherwise, they would watch her far too closely. She needed them off her back for the next couple of months.

"Of course," Berkowitz replied. "I'm sure you would have reported him if you had any idea before now." Liliana wasn't sure Berkowitz believed what either of them was saying. She tried to smile in agreement, but she was sure she ended up looking like she had gas or something.

"Mr Victor is being detained and any contact he may make is being monitored. If he tries to contact you, you'll be brought back for further questioning," Berkowitz reeled off. "If, in the meantime, Yates Ayad contacts you, please call the station." Liliana took the card Berkowitz handed over to her, detailing her direct line and email address.

"Thank you for coming down today. We'll be in contact, so please don't leave town." Berkowitz ended the interview and escorted Liliana back outside and into the sunshine.

Chapter Thirteen

The air outside the police station had never felt so fresh on her face. She hadn't realised how suffocating the station had felt until she was free from its grasp. Though she wasn't truly free, they would watch her. She did not know how she was going to continue with her plans with Yates with the police breathing down her neck.

Liliana wandered aimlessly down the street as she tried to come up with a plan going forward. She followed her feet back towards the city centre. She wound her way through the hustle and bustle. Most people were getting back to normal already. They trusted Sentinel had locked the bad guy up, that he was watching over them.

If only they knew.

She finally settled on getting herself a steaming hot latte while she thought out her next steps. She sat down outside a small café as she waited for her drink to arrive. She watched the citizens hurry past her, rushing off. The surrounding street was full of different businesses: a bookstore here, a clothes shop there, and right across the road from the café was an electronics shop. TV screens filled the shop window, showing various channels. One screen even showed a live feed of a camera pointed towards the street; she could see a small version of herself sitting outside the café.

The steaming hot latte distracted her for a moment. She thanked the server with a small smile before returning to watching the world carry on around her. One disruption soon followed another as the TV screens across the street blinked over to the same channel, one of the local news stations.

"Welcome to The News at Twelve. I am Joshua Harding," the newsreader introduced himself before shuffling the papers in front of him. *"The latest update from City Hall regarding the recent battle between Sentinel and Dark Warrior has revealed the identity of the Dark Warrior and his closest companions. Max Victor, the well-known tech mogul, was revealed to be the man behind the mask. His girlfriend, Liliana Masters, a journalist in our own city, has been avoiding the media ever since the battle took place."*

"Pinche mierda." They knew who she was. She would not get another job in her field ever again after this.

The reporter continued to report on her relationship with Max as they showed her photo alongside the live view.

"Avoiding the media, that is, until now. Liliana Masters has given an exclusive interview with our

own Tanya Netting. The interview, which is to be covered in the evening paper, shows Ms Masters denying any knowledge of Max Victor's secret identity. Although, one must wonder if what Ms Masters is saying is true, or is she trying to save her own back after they captured her boyfriend at the end of the battle that tore through our beloved city?"

With Liliana's picture glaring at her from across the street, she couldn't help but notice that the server, who was standing at the next table watching the news, was side-eyeing her. This was going to be her life now, being noticed for being the girlfriend of a known supervillain. Before anyone could say anything to her, Liliana stood and quickly stomped her way down the street and back to the apartment she shared with Max. She felt the need to hide out, away from prying eyes.

Her pace was a mistake. A mistake that was soon pointed out to her when even more people recognised her. A teenager with an obnoxious look on his pointed face shoved a phone camera into her face as she tried to walk past his group of friends.

"Why didn't you try to stop him?" the teenager asked, repeatedly stepping into her path to stop her from escaping his questioning. "How can you love a villain like Victor?"

"Leave me alone," she barked at the teenager, putting her hand up to the camera lens.

"Why didn't you call the police?" the teenager

shouted back, grabbing onto her arm as she tried to pass.

"I didn't know! Didn't you listen to the reporter?" Liliana yanked her arm out of his grip, which was painful given how weedy the kid was. Unexpectedly, the movement of her pulling away knocked the phone out of his other hand and sent it tumbling to the concrete slab they were standing on. Liliana was sure she heard a clink of broken glass as she stepped back, the teenager now shouting about his broken phone. It was his own fault; Liliana knew the brand broke repeatedly. She hurried off before he could shout some more at her, but she noticed some of his other friends had been recording them as well. Great, that was sure to make the rounds on YouTube later.

Liliana darted around the corner, leaving the teenager moaning about his broken phone to his friends, only to see some more curious citizens recognising her from the newscast. She was about to resign herself to being questioned all the way home when a compact car pulled up beside her. Yates was at the wheel.

"Quick, get in," Yates ordered, throwing open the passenger side door for her to jump in. They pulled away just as quickly as Yates had stopped. They were an excellent driver, even if they picked such a cramped car sometimes. "I saw the news. Safe to say your cover is blown."

"Recent interview, my ass. Tanya confronted me at work and tried to get anything she could out of me," Liliana replied, glad she no longer worked for the she-devil. "I don't think I'm going to show my face in the city for a while."

Even though she was a journalist herself, she never expected to be in the spotlight like this. Her face was on every screen as they drove past. Was this going to be her life now? All her experiences being boiled down to being the girlfriend of the bad guy. It just made her want to shout the truth about Max and Sentinel.

Yates was swerving through the city traffic with ease. They were an amazing driver. They cut off a couple people here and there but, oddly, no one seemed to mind very much. There was something about Yates that Liliana couldn't quite put her finger on. Before she could wonder very much, they took a sharp left turn, almost throwing Liliana about the car, with the seatbelt saving her at the last moment. She was quickly brought back to her current situation.

"What am I going to do, Yates? What can I do about this?" Liliana despaired.

"You can prepare for the mission." Yates was straight to the point. "Your life will not be the same again, although I think you already knew that."

She did. She felt it in the pit of her stomach. Her life as she knew it was over. She would now just be the girlfriend of a villain. Forever cast in Max's shadow. As much as she loved him, that didn't sit right with her. She would not live in his shadow. She needed to get ahead of this.

Her thoughts returned to the website she ran for several years. She had paid little attention to it in recent months, getting caught up between work and Max. Maybe it was time to bring it out of hiding again, start reporting on what's really going on in the city rather than letting the public believe what they were being spoon-fed by the Supers. It had been a while since she performed some real investigative journalism.

"I've collected some things from your apartment. I believe you won't want to stay there while this is all going on. I saw a group of paparazzi outside of your building as I left." Yates pointed towards the back seat which had two full duffle bags sat on them. "I hope you don't mind that I broke into your place."

"A small price to pay for avoiding the cameras, I suppose. Thanks," Liliana replied, balancing the pros and cons of the break-in. "Where are we heading?"

"Hilltop," Yates replied as they took the road out of the city towards Max's secret base. Liliana was still getting her head around the fact that Max had a secret base. "I cut the base off from the rest of the house without the passcode, we'll be safe there from the police."

Liliana breathed a sigh of relief when they left the city behind them, sinking into the seat of the car as the houses became more spread out around them. She could see a glint in the distance, the sunlight bouncing off the windows of Hilltop. The only thing that could convince her to relax fully was knowing that Max was going to be there waiting for her, if only that were possible.

"You won't have long to relax, I'm afraid." Yates pulled her attention back into the car.

"I'm sorry?" She replied.

"We have a lot of work to do if we are going to get Mr Victor back. We need to start a training regime. As far as I'm aware, you have little in the way of fighting skills. Or stealth." Yates seemed to appraise her as she was sitting in the car.

"Fair, I suppose. What do you have in mind?" Liliana asked, unsure if she wanted to hear the answer.

"Fighting. We're going to spar, and I'll teach you what I know," Yates replied. Somehow, that didn't help settle her nerves.

"Didn't you grow up fighting?"

"Yes, I did. Just means I've got more to teach." Yates turned and gave Liliana a smile that hinted at the bruises she would start collecting soon.

"Great."

Chapter Fourteen

She hit the mat hard. Although, she somehow broke nothing, yet.

"Again," Yates barked an order, standing over Liliana sprawled on the floor for the fiftieth time.

"Am I ever going to land a punch on you?" she groaned as Yates pulled her back to her feet.

"Maybe. If you improve." Yates stood back and fell into a fighting stance, which Liliana tried and failed to copy.

Yates darted forward and jabbed her in the side, Liliana moving to block herself far too late. She moved forward in response and missed Yates's shoulder, her fist flying instead. Yates grabbed her arm and flipped her over. She slammed into the mat yet again.

"Ow," Liliana whimpered slightly, rolling onto her side and into a ball to protect herself.

"You were closer that time," Yates stated, barely out of breath. "We'll take a break for today. We should get something to eat." They pulled Liliana up onto her feet again, and walked off the mat towards a side table with water bottles on it.

They were in the gym attached to Max's secret base. Someone fully equipped it, everything they could need to get Liliana into shape for the mission. Liliana hated the sight of the room now and they had only been training for two days. Yates had put her through a strict exercise routine from the moment Yates had brought her back to the base. Her picture was still all over the media, which just stirred her on to try harder with each sparring match Yates put her through.

It seemed cliché but the first thing she did once she reached the water table was spray her face with the freezing cold water. Messy but effective.

"Do some stretches before jumping in the shower. I'll get some food together," Yates ordered before walking back towards the kitchen. Liliana knew Yates worked for Max and not her, but they were rather bossy with the mission. It was a side she hadn't seen to Yates before. She groaned as she stretched out her sore muscles. She hoped she would see some improvement soon. She didn't know how many more beatings she could take.

She limped into the shower and let the boiling water run down her aching back, washing away the sweat she built up. She noticed some bruises forming on her stomach and sides, and she was sure one looked like a handprint on her arm where Yates flipped her repeatedly. Max had better appreciate everything she was doing for him. She would make sure he knew everything.

When she thought about seeing him again, she kept flipping between kissing him so hard she knocked the stuffing out of him or yelling at him about everything. She wasn't sure what she would do when she saw him again. She missed him. She loved and hated him, sometimes at the same time.

She couldn't help but imagine Max in the shower with her for a moment. Water rushing down their skin. The fight over, back in their happy place. She could almost feel his hands on her skin, running around her waist to stroke her back, pulling her in close.

But she couldn't let herself get distracted with what-ifs. It wasn't worth it. Focus.

She finished up in the shower and headed upstairs for some much-needed feeding. Yates was an incredible cook, although Liliana didn't always know what it was she was being fed. She didn't mind; the food was delicious.

After eating what Liliana was sure was a healthy meal, she took to exploring the complex built underneath Hilltop. There were corridors branching off corridors. She did not know how big it was, although she looked forward to exploring it. It was as if every additional room she discovered was a new aspect to the Max she was uncovering.

So far, she had found a room stocked with shelves

of papers and box files. A quick look at the papers told her they were research materials for new technological designs. She would need a dictionary at her side if she were to decode them.

After lunch, she found a new corridor to explore. The first room housed a reasonably sized pool. A pleasant surprise. It had been a while since she last went swimming. The next room pulled her in with its secrets. A large table, much like the one in the principal room she had just left, made for designing tools and technology. Lines crisscrossed the table with axes along the outside rim. A switch poked out of the side, prompting Liliana to press it. The table lit up.

"Is this where you make all your plans, Max?" Liliana asked the empty room. "How did you have time to do this?" she wondered. Looking to the side of the room, she saw racks of graph paper ready to be used for one design or another. A small desk stood next to the graph paper covered with pens, pencils, rulers, everything Max could need to make his designs.

"I see you found the design room."

Liliana's heart skipped a beat as she jumped a foot in the air, a high screech leaving her lips before she could stop it.

"Bloody hell, Yates. Don't sneak up on me like that."

"Sorry, Ms Masters." Although Yates didn't look sorry. In fact, they had a small smirk on their face, enjoying the shock they created.

"I was just exploring. I hope you don't mind," Liliana said.

"It's fine," Yates replied. "Mr Victor and I spent a far amount of time in this room. He designed the tech, I designed the suit."

"So, this is where all the brainstorming went on," Liliana said.

"And continues to go on. I've been experimenting with a design for you, Ms Masters," Yates said, surprising Liliana once more.

"For me? Why would I need a suit?" She thought she would simply wear dark clothing during the prison break.

"If all goes well, you shouldn't need a full fight suit," Yates replied. "But I think it's best we plan for the worst-case scenario." Liliana nodded. It made sense when she thought about it.

"I've taken the designs from Mr Victor's suit and made some improvements." Yates pulled some sheets from a storage slot underneath the table Liliana had missed. "It sounds bad, but with Mr Victor losing his fight, it has given me lots of feedback for improvements."

"I'm sure he'll appreciate hearing that," Liliana said with a small chuckle.

"I know," Yates said, holding back a smile. They laid out the sheets of graph paper on the bright table.

The drawings showed various designs, all based on a full-body suit like Max's. It had built in armour and space for weapons. Although she hoped she wouldn't need weapons on the mission.

"You've been busy."

"I don't sleep much," Yates replied, not very forthcoming on the personal details, as per the usual. "The plans still need some work. If you have any requests, I can see about working some in if you like."

"How about a cape? Or would that look stupid because I can't fly?" Liliana was getting ahead of herself. The idea of having a superhero suit was mildly intoxicating. She just had to remember that she didn't have any powers, and if she was going to be fighting anyone, it was likely to be the apparent good guys.

Was she becoming a villain? Liliana shook her head. That was a question for another day.

"No capes," Yates said, looking Liliana right in the eyes. "They look stupid and aren't practical. Only for show."

"Oh," Liliana replied. She felt like she was being told off by her old schoolteacher.

"If I have time, I can see about adding a little flare if it's really important to you. But no capes."

"Okay. Thank you for all of this, Yates."

Chapter Fifteen

Liliana kept the self-torture going and switched the TV on, only to see her own face staring back at her again. They were still running the ambush of an interview she had been through a couple days before. She hated being at the centre of attention like this. What she needed to do was defer the focus off her, even if it put it back on Max. She couldn't carry on with the mission with all eyes on her.

As she sat on the sofa, trying to make a plan, she noticed her laptop resting on the coffee table at her side. Ideas sprang forward. If she needed to separate herself from Max, there was only one place to start, only one place the idiots in the city might actually believe her. Social media. She flipped the laptop open and hit the power button. She hated what she was about to do, but needs must. She opened her various social media accounts and changed her profile, showing herself to be single. She removed Max from all mention on her accounts.

Her heart raced as her accounts asked her if she was sure of the changes she was making, showing her Max's profile picture. As if she needed reminding of their date night from a few months before. Max managed to get a half-decent photo of them both as she sat on a balcony overlooking the city. She clicked to confirm the changes as her heart broke once more.

"If you want to make it one hundred percent clear you've broken off with Mr Victor, you could make it look like his betrayal turned you off of men altogether," Yates said from behind Liliana.

"You really need to stop creeping up on me like that," Liliana said, almost jumping out of her skin at Yates's voice.

"My apologies. I don't do it on purpose," Yates replied.

"But you have a good point," Liliana went back into her profile settings and changed her interests from men and women to just women. "Do you have any other suggestions?"

"I think it might be best if you made it look like you were going along with your normal routine," Yates replied, sitting on the chair across from Liliana.

"I can't really do that after getting fired," Liliana pointed out dryly.

"Of course. But you could start looking for a new job, you could go out to eat, meet up with your friends. Even Rose," Yates suggested.

"A fruitless endeavour. I'm sure no one will want to

hire me at the moment," Liliana said. "But it would be good for appearance's sake, I suppose."

Resigned to her new course of action, she opened a document on her laptop that she hadn't had to use for some time. Her CV.

"Better freshen up my CV, then."

"I'll make coffee," Yates said, walking towards the kitchen.

"You're amazing, Yates," Liliana called after them.

*

The next morning, Liliana drove into town. Yates had lent her the compact car they used for city life. Liliana made a point of returning to her flat, if only to clear it out. While she wanted to fool the press into thinking she had given Max up, she didn't like the idea of them knowing where she lived. Her plan was to make it look like she had got herself a new place to live, away from prying eyes, but she was just going to be staying at the base until they got Max back.

She glimpsed a half-dozen reporters and cameras waiting outside her building as she passed them to get to the building's parking lot.

"Here we go," she groaned to herself, grabbing her bag as she braced herself to power walk through the press.

"Liliana!"

"Ms Masters, have you heard from your boy-friend?"

"Why did you change your relationship status?"

"Have you turned gay?"

The reporters shouted over each other as she tried to get to her front door and leave them behind. The flash of the cameras almost blinded her as she fumbled with her keys. She managed to slot the key in as she told the press to leave her alone. She quickly slammed the door behind her, stopping anyone from forcing their way in behind her. She thanked whatever god was listening for the heavily tinted windows on the building's front doors. The press couldn't see her flushed face and tearful eyes. Being on this side of the news wasn't anywhere near as fun as being the reporter. She suddenly found herself grateful that she harassed no one like that. At least she didn't think she had been that kind of reporter. She hoped she hadn't.

She dragged her feet towards the three flights of steps facing her. Someone had broken the elevator about a week after she moved in. It never seemed to get fixed for more than a couple of hours. It was good for exercise, though. The night before, Liliana arranged for movers to come pack up her apartment and put it all in a storage container she had rented. She just wanted to grab the essentials before heading out to show her face in public, conveniently, in front of cameras.

She unlocked her apartment door in a much less rushed manner, only to see someone sat on her sofa.

"What is it with people being in my home without me? First the police, now you," Liliana complained half-heartedly.

"Sorry, but I knew you would come back here at some point and I wanted to see you," Rose apologised, standing up to hug Liliana.

It felt good to hug Rose again. A small amount of normalcy in the weird world that was her life now.

"It's good to see you, Rose." Liliana gave her a squeeze before stepping back to drop her bag on the coffee table.

"How are you doing?" Rose asked, a concerned look crossing her face.

"As well as can be considered," Liliana replied conservatively. Rose was her best friend and Liliana wanted to tell her everything, but she also wanted to keep her out of trouble. Rose had come out of the scandal relatively unscathed. Who was Liliana to drag her down with her?

"I saw what you did last night. Your relationship status," Rose said. It was obvious that she wanted to ask questions about it. She was inquisitive, yet never wanted to cross a boundary. "Are you sure you're okay?"

"I'm fine, Rose. I've just been thinking about it all."

Liliana wanted to avoid lying outright to Rose if she could help it.

Rose narrowed her eyes at Liliana's reply, wanting more information. She sat on the arm of the sofa, facing her. Liliana just noticed how tense Rose was. Her shoulders were tight, raised slightly. Her jaw clenched, grinding her teeth.

"Are you okay, Rose?" Liliana moved forward to rest her hand on Rose's tense shoulders. A glint out of the window distracted her momentarily. The sun bounced off of something familiar.

It all clicked together. At the same moment, Liliana's jaw dropped slightly, and Rose shook her head slowly. She was being watched by more than just the press. Sentinel was outside. Liliana panicked internally. She was nowhere near ready for a confrontation; she didn't have any weapons on her. No gear.

"I'm fine, Lils. Just a lot on my plate." Rose brought her attention back to the present, not the potential future. Neither of them could be honest with each other. Sentinel could hear them if he focused hard enough. Was he watching Liliana? Rose? Both of them? They couldn't be sure.

"Okay. Let me know if there is anything I can do," Liliana said, hoping Rose caught her double meaning.

"I will. You have enough going on yourself. Job hunting, giving up men altogether. Busy week,"

Rose tried to joke, making Liliana crack a small smile. Rose was getting her sarcasm back, bit by bit.

"Know of any jobs for me?" Liliana asked, trying to keep the tone light. She grabbed a suitcase from her hallway cupboard and packed some clothes, books, and pictures.

"Well, you could always apply for your old job. It would put a funny look on Tanya's face," Rose chuckled. Liliana just raised her eyebrow in response.

"Maybe once things have settled down, it'll be easier," Liliana replied.

"For the job or for your love life?" Rose asked.

"Both," Liliana laughed at herself.

For a moment there, it almost felt like they were back to normal.

"Do you want to get a drink?" Liliana asked.

"That sounds like a great idea," Rose sighed. They both grabbed their bags and Liliana's suitcase, and headed back out of the apartment.

"Vinnie's sound okay to you?" Liliana asked as they walked down the stairs.

"That's on the other side of town. You sure you want to go that far?" Rose replied.

"It's not one of our normal spots so the cameras shouldn't follow us there," Liliana explained. "I have a car downstairs so it shouldn't take us too long to get there."

"Okay, fair enough," Rose replied.

Rose was much less afraid to get rough with the press if needed. She barged her way through the group of cameras and pulled Liliana through behind her. It didn't take long to get past them and into the parking lot.

"Nice car. Where did you get it?" Rose asked as Liliana loaded the suitcase into the boot of the car.

"Thanks, it's just a rental." That wasn't a complete lie. She was borrowing it from Yates, she just wasn't paying for it.

They sat in slightly awkward silence as they travelled across town. Occasionally, they drove past a screen showing the news, showing photos from outside her apartment building. They would not leave her alone. Thankfully, they didn't seem to get a good photo of her car, so they couldn't track where she was going. They pulled up outside Vinnie's in time to see the closest screen switch over to a recorded montage of Sentinel working in the city, lifting concrete and talking to citizens. Liliana would not watch, but she saw a familiar flash of red hair show up on the screen.

"Rose. I didn't know you spoke to Sentinel," Liliana said. Rose was immediately put on edge once again.

"Yeah. He was helping the builders working on our office building when I left work the other day." She fidgeted, rubbing her hands around and around. "He just started talking to me. Wanted to know about you." Rose's eyes darted around as she spoke, looking towards the sky. She made Liliana wonder if Sentinel was still watching. Close enough to hear every word they spoke, but far enough so they couldn't see him. Powers work to his benefit, and to their cost.

"Should we go inside? Get some drinks?" Liliana opened the bar door and followed Rose in.

A wall of thunderous noise hit them as soon as they pulled the inside door open. The latest hits blared out of a dozen speakers placed strategically around the bar.

Liliana shouted over the din to Rose, telling her to find them a table while she grabbed them some drinks. She watched Rose disappear into the crowd as she fought her way to the bar.

"Two glasses of rosé, please," Liliana shouted across the busy bar, handing over some cash. She glanced over her shoulder while she waited for the wine, trying to see where Rose had ended up. Several flashes of red hair caught her eye, none of them belonging to her redhead.

"Here you go," the bartender shouted across to Liliana, drawing her attention back to their drinks. "Hang on, you're her, aren't you? The Dark Warrior's girlfriend." The bartender recognised her.

"Nope," Liliana lied before darting off into the crowd, hoping the bartender would not follow up on his questions.

It was situations like this one where she hated being as short as she was. The crowd surrounding her stood head and shoulders above her. It reduced her to peeking through arms to find Rose. Eventually she thought she spotted her best friend sitting at a table against the back wall. Liliana noticed something that immediately put her in a foul mood, or one worse than she was already in. Rose wasn't alone at the table.

"Timmy. What are you doing here?" Liliana interrupted whatever he was saying to Rose. Liliana passed over the wine, noting that Rose was impossibly tense in Tim's presence.

"Ah, the villain's girl. Surprised to see you out in public," Tim replied, raising his eyebrows at Liliana's appearance.

"Why shouldn't I be out in public? I've not done anything wrong," Liliana replied.

"No?" Tim asked. "Some people would say differently. Max was supposedly the love of your life, or something like that." He had the audacity to chuckle as he said those words.

"So you can imagine how much of a surprise this all has been. Even for me. Especially for me."

Liliana was doing her best to not let Tim get her all riled up, but it was hard.

"Still. You're all over the media. You should read some of the blog posts about you out on the web," Tim replied. He was actively trying to get a rise out of her.

"What happened to our girls' night?" She turned to Rose, deciding to ignore Tim. She turned to face Rose head on, trying to block Tim from their conversation.

"Sorry. He just came up to me as soon as I sat down," Rose sighed. "There weren't any other tables, I didn't want to lose this one. Even to him."

"Ignore me if you want. But I'm right." Tim edged himself back into view. "You're out of a job. No one wants to hire you right now. You need my connections." He was quickly changing from annoying to a bragging idiot. Liliana ended this conversation once and for all.

"Tim," she locked eyes with him, wanting to make sure her point got across, "your connections mean shit to me. You're as useful as a decaf espresso"— she leaned in to finish her sentence—"now leave us alone." She pointed away from their table, raising her voice, hoping others surrounding them would hear her.

"Is this man bothering you, miss?" a mountain of a man turned around from the neighbouring table. What appeared to be his wife stood next to him, staring Tim down, somehow seeming more menacing than the Hulk of a man she was with.

"Don't worry, we're all friends here." Tim tried to get rid of the scary couple.

"No, we're not," Rose replied shortly.

"You need to leave," the woman ordered. She had a calm yet terrifying way of speaking. Chills ran down Liliana's spine at her voice. Surprisingly, Tim wasn't already running for the hills. She would be if she were him.

Tim stared down the couple for a moment more before shrugging his shoulders in defeat and walking away from the group. Rose couldn't hold it in anymore, she burst out laughing.

"I'm sorry. But you guys are amazing. Thank you," Rose said between laughs.

"No worries. You let us know if he comes back again," the impossibly large man said, his tone now deep and pleasing to the ear, no sense of hostility remaining.

"Thank you. You saved us from some very frustrating arguments," Liliana said, smiling at the couple as they turned back to their drinks.

"I thought I might have got rid of him now I'm not a journalist anymore," Liliana said, taking a sip of her wine.

"Don't say that." Rose tapped her on the arm. "You're still a journalist. You just need to find a new place to work."

"Yeah? Who's going to hire the girlfriend of the bad guy?" Liliana asked, already knowing the answer.

"They'll come around. Just give them time," Rose replied. "Tanya might even ask you back once everything dies down a little."

"Ha. Like Tanya would ever go back on one of her decisions."

"It could happen," Rose tried to convince her.

"If pigs could fly, Rose."

The two of them laughed together for an hour or two before deciding to call it a night. Neither of them noticed the phones pointed in their direction, strangers taking pictures of the villain's girlfriend out with a friend.

Chapter Sixteen

Liliana woke the next morning, hangover free thankfully, only to see new pictures of herself on the news. These were from her drinks with Rose. So much for the safety of being on the opposite side of the city from her usual haunts.

"Ms Liliana Masters, the former girlfriend of Max Victor, also known as Dark Warrior, was spotted socialising last night," the reporter read from his notes as they scrolled through photos from the night before. "These pictures, combined with the latest information from her social media accounts, would seem to suggest that she is denying all knowledge of Victor's alter ego."

They were finally getting the point. Liliana breathed a sigh of relief. She hoped they would now lose interest in her.

"Sources have told this station that the woman who accompanied Ms Masters in these pictures is Ms Rose Wilson, a long-time friend and former colleague of Ms Masters." The reporter shuffled his papers as he spoke. He was trying to sound like he was reporting on major issues, not the social life of a diminishing public figure. "Given the latest information from social media,

could this friendship be developing into something more? Ms Wilson is known in social circles to be of the homosexual persuasion, could she be turning Ms Masters?"

"TURNING?" Liliana shouted at the television. "What kind of crap is this? Are we in the twentieth century or something?"

"He was always a backward idiot." Yates walked into the room to hear Liliana screaming at the screen.

"I never noticed it before now, but you're right. Backwards idiot." Liliana angrily shut off the TV.

"At least your plan seems to be working."

"I suppose. The media frenzy should die down now," Liliana said.

"Fingers crossed," Yates replied.

The computer behind the pair dinged, drawing their attention away from the now blank television. Yates went over to check the notification that had popped up on the security screen.

"We've got mail," Yates said before walking away towards the secret door linking the base with Hilltop.

"Mail? From who?" Liliana said, confused. "Who knows we're here to send us mail?" Yates walked off before giving Liliana an answer, leaving her amid confusion.

A couple of minutes later, Yates returned with a small, flat package. They turned it over in their hands, brow furrowed in contemplation.

"Who's it from?" Liliana asked.

"Mr Victor," Yates replied, stunning Liliana.

"How?" Yet more confusion. "How on earth has he sent something while under lock and key?"

"I am unsure," Yates replied. "He has made many friends over the years, it is possible one could do this favour for him."

Liliana held out her hand. Surely the package was for her, she thought. Yates kept hold of it.

"It's addressed to me, Ms Masters."

"Oh. Okay." Liliana wasn't sure what to make of that. She hoped Max would have found a way to contact her. She needed to speak to him. Too many questions remained on her mind. Yates turned the package over in their hands for a moment more before ripping it open. A letter fell out into Yates's open hand.

"What has he said?" Liliana knew she was being rude, but she needed to know. Yates unfolded the letter and read aloud.

"Dear Yates,

It would appear you may have been right.

I know you will enjoy reading me admitting that; it doesn't happen very often, after all. I hope you are keeping well and aren't planning anything ridiculous. I made mistakes and am now paying for them.

The guards here take great pleasure in telling me the details of the aftermath. The damage I caused. The people I killed.

No.

I didn't kill them. He did.

I didn't want a fight. I only wanted to protect Liliana. I didn't want to hurt anyone. Except maybe Sentinel. But you know how I feel about that so-called man.

What hurts the most is knowing how I betrayed her. I should have told her the truth. I know that now. But I've lost her. I saw the news this morning. She's moving on. I understand. It hurts, but I understand.

I wanted to thank you for everything you've done for me. For your kind friendship. I believe this is the end of our journey.

I wish you all the best for the future.

May we meet again.

Max"

For the first time, she saw Yates break a little. A tear broke free from their eye and landed on the letter in their hands.

"He's saying goodbye," Liliana said to herself more than anything. "He believes that I've not forgiven him. Oh god, I didn't think it would be this hard." Liliana's heart hurt as she realised how alone Max must feel. She sat back on the arm of the chair behind her, clutching at her chest.

Yates shook their head, wiping the tear away before more could join it.

"This was bound to happen. I didn't think he would get word out so quickly, but if he believes the lie, then surely everyone else must," Yates said, folding the letter away into their inside pocket.

"Can we reply?" Liliana asked, wishing she could make Max feel better somehow.

"Not without it going through official channels. I don't know who his contact is. He didn't say," Yates replied. Liliana's shoulders dropped in resignation. After a pause Liliana stood, took in a deep breath, and marched out of the room, down to the gym.

"What are you doing?" Yates called after her.

"Training," she replied. "We need to get Max out as soon as possible."

Yates nodded. They followed Liliana's train of thought and her path to the gym. They needed to get down to work.

*

Yet again, Liliana slammed into the mat. She was sure most of her back was black and blue by now. Yates walked her through some more fighting moves before trying them out for practice. Liliana spent most of her time on the floor, struggling to fight back. They were too fast.

"Again," Yates ordered, kicking Liliana back onto her feet. Liliana was quickly tiring of Yates's attitude while sparring. It was as if they didn't see the difference between practice and actual life. She half expected Yates to knock her out at some point.

Liliana stood, feet apart, knees slightly bent, fists raised. Ready for the attack. She watched Yates; they stood calmly, apparently unprepared for the fight. Their next move wasn't clear until a split second before it happened. All Liliana wanted to do was land a hit, and maybe stay on her feet for once. Then Liliana remembered something she had seen on TV the other week, a specific move that would render your opponent's arm dead in the water. You couldn't trust everything you saw on TV, but she hoped this one move might actually help her.

Yates suddenly moved forward, their right hand made into a fist, aiming at Liliana's battered head. Deciding to try the new move, Liliana sidestepped, palm against Yates's fist, and hit the underside of their upper arm. Yates's arm fell flat against their side, their face a picture of surprise.

"What?" Their mouth fell open in shock. "Where did you learn that?"

Liliana laughed in surprise. "It worked!" She jumped back before Yates could attempt to hit her with their left hand.

"Tell me, where did you learn that?" Yates repeated themselves.

"Thank you, Netflix!" Liliana exclaimed, arms raised in celebration.

Yates slowly started regaining feeling in their arm and flexed their hand a little. They stared down at their arm, trying to figure out what just happened. While Liliana hadn't planted Yates on the mat this time, it couldn't be denied that she won that bout.

"Well done, Ms Masters."

"I told you to call me Liliana." Yates just ignored her request once again.

"Take a five-minute break, then start some reps on the programme I gave you the other day."

"So, you won't use my first name, but you will give me orders. Odd." Liliana raised an eyebrow at Yates before they walked away, smirking.

Liliana grabbed a bottle of water from the mini fridge standing against the back wall of the gym. She glanced over at the exercise plan laid out on a nearby table, reminding herself what she needed to do. That last fight had improved her mood somewhat. It helped to know that she was improving. Maybe she could trip Yates up in their next fight. Although that might just be wishful thinking.

Chapter Seventeen

After running through the exercises, Liliana walked through the complex, trying to see what Yates had disappeared to do earlier that afternoon. She eventually found them in the design room, hunched over the lit-up table, various plans scattered around them. Liliana stepped over a couple pieces of paper, some scrunched up, to move to the opposite side of the table to Yates.

"What are you up to in here?" she asked.

"Oh, Ms Masters, I didn't hear you come in." Yates looked up in surprise.

"How the tables have turned," Liliana chuckled.

"I'm working on the design for your suit. The right combinations seem to elude me" Yates turned back to the sheets of paper in front of them.

Liliana looked over the papers, each one showing a different aspect of the suit. It was all very complicated. She didn't envy Yates's self-appointed task.

"Need any help?" she asked, hoping Yates asked nothing too technical from her.

"Your measurements, actually." Yates looked her

up and down. They pulled open a drawer and took out a small device Liliana didn't recognise.

"What's that?" she asked.

"Stand against that wall, please," Yates ordered, switching the device on. It had a small screen pointed towards the user, with a horizontal slit pointed towards Liliana. She nervously moved as instructed. "Arms stretched out." Liliana complied.

Yates raised the device and pointed it directly at Liliana's head. They went to pull the worryingly gun-like trigger, making Liliana close her eyes and wince, waiting for something that never came. She peeked through one eye to see that the device was a scanner.

"Oh. That's what it does," Liliana said, relieved, if nothing else.

Yates waved the scanner over Liliana's body, motioning for her to turn on the spot as required.

"All done. Now I can model the suit on a scan of you. That should help," Yates said, a glint of excitement in their eyes.

"That didn't feel invasive at all," Liliana remarked. She brushed herself down and left Yates to their work. They seemed engaged in the design process, anyway.

*

After yet another training session, this one solo,

Liliana put her mind to work as well as her body. She found some research notes of Max's. He was trying to find the secret identities of the city's heroes: Sentinel, Lightbringer and Glassier. The so-called holy trinity. Max had files of varying thickness on the three of them. His focus seemed to be Sentinel. On the other hand, he had barely any information on Glassier. Considering he or she was an invisible hero, that was no surprise.

Sentinel's dossier was full of photos, mainly from the press. He did like to show off for the camera. Tall, dark and cocky. He was rarely seen without a smile unless it was an action shot. Then he was focused, too focused for Liliana's liking. It was all for show.

Max kept logs of his appearances. The records were actually giving off a creepy stalker vibe.

"Oh, Max. Be glad the authorities never found these," Liliana said to no one in particular. She continued to flick through the file and found some scientific reports that she didn't completely understand. They looked like tracking reports.

"What were you doing, Max?"

Was he trying to track Sentinel mid-flight? Trying to find his base of operations, or his home?

"Serious stalker vibes now." It was creepy yet understandable. That was an intensely confusing feeling for Liliana. It wasn't right to stalk someone like this, but Sentinel was a danger to the people.

Did that make this right?

Another in a long line of questions and discussion topics once she got in front of Max again. She had to admit to herself, she often came across a feeling of doubt in her current plan of action. She was woefully unprepared for this task. Part of her wished she had never bumped into Max that day. Of course, a moment after thinking that, she was washed over with guilt.

Liliana rubbed her eyes, trying to work through the confusion and frustration. Why did Max have to carry this weight on his shoulders? Why was it his responsibility? Why was it now hers?

Even for a journalist, she hadn't had this many questions in a long time. Not since she noticed how hot Julia Stanton was in high school. That had thrown her through a loop, one that took her 4 years and a brief fling with Julia to understand fully.

Her life in high school. That got her thinking. Surely Sentinel, or rather his alter ego, attended some sort of schooling system. He has already stated that he wasn't an alien, born and bred human, just with a few extra talents. So, he was a kid; he went through puberty. That surely messed with his powers, along with everything else.

Liliana brought the pictures of Sentinel back into the light, taking a good look at his smug face. He didn't look to be much older than her and Max.

Liliana ran and grabbed her laptop from her room and quickly started looking at archived newspapers, both national and on the local level. If something went wrong with his powers as a teenager, it might have made the news.

"See, Max, you should have spoken to me sooner. You're not the only one with specific abilities," Liliana laughed as she finally felt like she had caught a break. She was on her way to finding out who Sentinel was. That might just come in handy down the line.

*

Rose couldn't help feeling that she was being watched. She'd felt eyes following her for days now, and she was almost certain it was one specific pair of eyes. Sentinel. He was following her, waiting for her to mess up and reveal something she didn't even know.

She had no privacy, and she hated it.

She hadn't even undressed fully since the watching began, switching from underwear to swimsuit ungracefully in an attempt to not reveal anything. It was exhausting. Yet, sleep eluded her.

Gulping down her third coffee of the morning, Rose found a small desk in one of the many tents Tanya had set up outside of the half destroyed office building. Rose wondered how long they were going to be working in tents. She thought a new workspace would have been a top priority, but no.

Tents were what they had.

She plugged in her laptop and started transferring the latest batch of photos she had taken around the city. The focus of her team lately was on the rebuilding efforts around the city. People pulling together to get back to normal. It was a fluff piece built into a major story. Tanya tasked Rose with capturing the various efforts across the city.

"Ah, Rose. There you are," a shrill voice called over to her desk. Tanya was pushing her way through the desks to get to her. "I've been waiting for you to come in." She was actually early, but sure.

"What can I do for you?" Rose asked, dreading the answer.

"I need to speak to you about Ms Masters," Tanya said. Of course, this was about Liliana.

"What about her?" Rose replied.

"I am aware you are friends outside of work," Tanya began. "I need to know what you spoke about the other night. Does she know anything more about Max Victor?"

"You want me to report on my friendship?" Rose asked, her brow creased in a frown.

"No. I want you to do your job and report on the important news stories of the day," Tanya barked. "Like it or not, Ms Masters is important to the current events, and you have a unique insight into her mind. Does she know anything else about Max?"

Tanya asked again.

"No. She doesn't. She knows what kind of man he turned out to be so she's distancing herself from him," Rose replied, lying through her teeth. She knew it wasn't that simple for Liliana, and she suspected she wasn't quite done with Max. But with eyes watching and Tanya listening, she couldn't very well throw her best friend to the hungry wolves. Not until Liliana knew of what she was doing and what consequences were coming her way.

Tanya didn't look convinced by Rose's answer.

"So, are the two of you hooking up, then? Like the reporter suggested last night?"

"That's none of your business. Even if it were true," Rose retorted.

"It is my business if one of my employees goes and gets involved with the front-page story of the day," Tanya replied, either unaware of how inappropriate she was being or she just simply didn't care.

"No, it's really not. In any case, we are just friends." Rose almost said that they had dated before but it didn't work out. But that was just adding fuel to the flame.

Tanya narrowed her eyes at being told off by Rose. They stared at each other for a moment, each waiting for the other to say something else. For once, Rose wasn't willing to back down to Tanya. She needed to protect herself and Liliana. Protect their friendship.

"Fine. I believe you. For now," Tanya finally broke. "Get to work. The new starter will be here soon. I'll need you to show him the ropes," she ordered as she walked off.

Well, that order came out of nowhere. One minute Rose was being interrogated and the next it was business as normal. Rose looked forward to the day she could finally quit and move on with her life, away from Tanya. Although she did occasionally fantasize about one day being Tanya's replacement.

She delved into her work for a time, thinking about a rose-coloured day where she could get rid of Tanya. Because of the need for gritty, real-life photos for the story, the pictures she uploaded needed little work. She finished a lot sooner than she thought she would, just hitting save to the last picture as it found its way onto the office cloud.

"You'll be sitting here, next to the best photographer in the business." Tanya's annoying voice made its way back to Rose. It shocked her to hear Tanya give Rose a compliment; she must be trying to impress the new reporter.

Rose sucked in a deep breath and turned to great the newcomer.

"What are you doing here?" she blurted out before she could stop herself.

"Hello there, Rosie," Tim smirked down at Rose.

"Ah, you two know each other. Brilliant," Tanya smiled. "I'll leave you to show Mr Westfield how we do things around here." She hurried off before Rose could object. Tim grabbed a nearby chair and pulled it up to the space next to Rose.

"So, how do you do things around here?" Tim asked sarcastically. Rose groaned and rubbed her eyes.

Chapter Eighteen

Job hunting sucked. It sucked hard. It starkly reminded Liliana why she stuck at her last job despite the horrid boss. She'd updated her CV and updated her social media pages. Nothing. Application after application. Whenever they deigned to give her a response, it was an overly polite rejection.

While she knew it had only been a couple of days, and she didn't really want a new job, it was disheartening. If she weren't actually planning a prison break, Max's defeat would have ruined her career in this city. She shared a quick post lamenting her rejections, she had to keep up the charade of trying to move on with her life, and logged off the computer.

Leaning back on the sofa, the laptop moved to her side, she rubbed her eyes. Once again faced with a tough reality. Her body ached, drained from a day of training and job hunting. The two halves of her world smashing against each other, each vying for attention just at the wrong times. She needed to unwind.

Of course, her usual method of relaxation was unavailable to her. Locked up in a prison several miles away. Max always knew what to do, how to help her unwind after a tough day at work.

*

Liliana slammed the door behind her as she walked through the entryway of Max's flat. Throwing her bag at a random chair, she let out a huff of exasperation.

"Rough day?" Max asked, coming out of the kitchen. He was carrying two glasses of wine.

"You have no idea," Liliana replied, thankfully taking the glass that was offered to her.

"Go ahead and rant, you know you want to," Max said, smiling at her annoyingly.

Liliana took in a deep breath and let out her frustrations.

"She is refusing to fire him!" she started.

"Who?" Max asked.

"Walter. The new intern," she replied. "He screws everything up and won't admit he's wrong. She doesn't see it." Of course, she was referring to Tanya, the she-devil in charge of the paper.

"Tanya's not the type to let screw-ups go unpunished," Max said, furrowing his brow in confusion.

"Not normally. But Walter can get away with anything." Liliana paced the living room, gulping down her wine mid-rant. "All because Tanya is screwing his rich daddy." Comprehension showed on Max's face.

"Ah. So, he has a free pass."

"Until Tanya moves onto the next unsuspecting victim," Liliana admitted. Max nodded along with her rant. "Normally, I could ignore his stupidity. But not today."

"What happened today?" Max asked.

"The boy cancelled half my appointments on my calendar before I even had a chance to double check everything this morning, so I missed several important interviews," Liliana half shouted in frustration. "Do you have any idea how unprofessional that made me look? I ended up spending my lunch break chasing everyone down to apologise and reschedule." She took another gulp of wine.

"That sucks, Lils." Max stood to rub her shoulders, trying to help her calm down. She just kept pacing, moving out of his reach every so often.

"Damn right it sucks. I could even see that it was him that made the mistakes. The edit log literally had his name all over it. Do you think he admitted he was wrong?"

"I'm guessing not."

"Of course not. He just shrugged his shoulders and walked away from me. Smug asshole." She let out another huff of exasperation before slumping down onto the annoyingly comfortable sofa.

"Given Tanya's track record, it shouldn't be too long before the guy gets fired. Then we'll celebrate if you like." Max sat down next to Liliana, trying to cheer her up.

"That'll be nice," she replied, leaning her head on his muscular arm.

Max leaned over and kissed the top of Liliana's head, his warm breath flowing down her hair, caressing the back of her neck.

Liliana sighed contently as she took in the scent of Max's cologne. Faded since that morning, but just powerful enough to put a smile on her formerly stressed face.

Max wrapped his arms around her shoulders, pulling her in close. He gently tipped her face up to his, a finger under her chin, moving her closer.

"You're sexy when you get all riled up. You know that, right?" Max whispered in his deep tone. Before she could respond, Max closed the gap between them and kissed her. Deeply, passionately. He stole her breath away and woke her body up all in one moment.

She remembered to put her wine down this time. No more distractions. Liliana twisted to kneel on the sofa, using her hands to cup Max's face, refusing to break the contact their lips had made.

Brushing Max's dark locks away from his face, Liliana returned his kiss, eager for more. For release.

Max's hands drifted down from Liliana's face. Down her side, gently grazing the sides of her breasts. Down past her waist, coming to grip her hips tightly. He *guided her to sit across him, which she did happily.*

Their kiss deepened. Liliana wasn't sure how, but it did. She ran her hands through Max's soft hair as she felt him explore her body. She pressed herself against Max, as close as she could get. Only their clothes holding them apart.

Max broke the kiss first, pausing to look up into her eyes, pushing her long hair away, letting the light shine against her tawny skin. "Gorgeous," he said simply before bringing her back down for another kiss. She responded by moving her hips slowly, but firmly, against him. It only took a second before she could feel him reacting. Max groaned into her kiss and moved his hot lips to kiss down her neck, prompting Liliana to move her hips some more. She could tell Max was aching to move with her. But he seemed to enjoy what she was doing too much to change.

Still running her hands through Max's hair, she pulled tightly, making him kiss her again. He loved it when she took charge. As a reward, she moved against him, rougher than before. That was his breaking point. He pulled Liliana's dress above her head, leaving her in her underwear. He twisted, throwing her down on the sofa, taking back control.

He left a trail of kisses down her neck and across her flushed chest. As he kissed her, he lifted her hips slightly and pulled her underwear down. Next, he slid a hand in between Liliana and the sofa, undoing her bra clasp. Soon her body was fully exposed, while he knelt above her, yet to remove a single item. She could feel his gaze moving all over, taking in the sight of her body, laid bare. She looked up at him as he had the goofiest smile on his face, as if they hadn't done this before.

Neither of them said a word as he finally lifted his t-shirt over his head and threw it to the floor with her clothes. His lightly toned torso was in shadow as the light shone behind him, making the edge of his muscular arms glow slightly.

He unbuckled his trousers and lent back down to kiss Liliana again. She took the chance and ran her hands up and down Max's sides, memorising the feel of him pressed against her, free of clothes. After another heat-filled kiss, Max returned to kissing down Liliana, taking his time to move down her body. Liliana moaned as he dipped down to her stomach. She could feel his chest hovering above a rather sensitive area. She couldn't decide if she wanted him to continue downward or to come back up so she could wrap her legs around him. Although she could do that either way, she supposed.

Max leant against her as he kicked off his trousers, finally. She got a brief feeling of contact with her before he moved down. His hands gripped her hips, stopping her from trying to rise for more. He chuckled as he noticed how worked up she was getting. He teased her by gently running his hands between her legs, making her gasp and moan once more.

"Patience, my love," he said, still smiling that goofy grin. He returned to kissing, now down to her hips, just above his hands. Her hands were gripping the sofa in anticipation. He hovered above her, his breath leaving her tingling and wriggling for contact. He peeked up at her before his mouth finally made contact. Liliana moaned in pleasure.

Max held her down while he devoured her. Liliana barely held back from screaming as Max let his tongue go to work. Liliana didn't think it could get any better, but then she felt one of his hands drift down to join his mouth. He slid a finger in where his tongue just couldn't reach, taking Liliana over the edge, into oblivion. He gently massaged her as she rode out the orgasm, only just holding back from holding his head down there.

As she came down from the high, Max pulled away to grab a small foil packet from the trousers strewn on the floor. Liliana normally thought it presumptuous that he carried them with him. Not today. Today she was grateful he had one so close.

Once he was protected, he lay above Liliana, hovering once again. "Ready?" he asked.

"More than ready," Liliana replied, aching for him to be closer. He lent down to kiss her as he lined up and gently slid inside her. They groaned together as they revelled in the sensation.

Their kiss grew stronger as Max moved, making full use of his size. Liliana wrapped her arms around his waist, running her hands across his back as he moved. She could feel the pressure building again. He dipped his head down to kiss her neck, to the sensitive spot only he knew to find. Her back arched against Max as she went over the edge once more, unable to stop the scream that time.

As she came down from the high once again, she pushed Max back to climb on top of him. He sat against the back of the sofa and used the freedom to run his hands anywhere he could reach. Liliana lowered herself down onto him, kissing him to capture his moan. It was her turn to be in control, and she enjoyed it. She liked to explore Max's enticing body, finding new ways to elicit reactions from him.

Liliana lent back slightly to run her hands down Max's chest. He took the opportunity to do the same. He cupped her breasts as she moved against him. The goofy grin had disappeared, replaced with wonder and wilderment. She let him explore for a minute before she fully took charge. She took his hands and pinned them against the wall above them. He could easily move, if he truly wanted to, but he loved being the sub occasionally.

Holding their hands together up high, Liliana moved up and down beside Max. She could feel herself slowly building again, and going by the sound of Max's breathing, he was doing the same. The more they built, the more restless Max became underneath her. His hips bucked into her as he struggled to control himself. Liliana enjoyed watching Max wriggle be-

neath her. It was interesting, the powerful sensation. She knew she could bring Max to his knees with ecstasy if she wanted to. He could truly let go with her. He trusted her fully, and she felt the same. Trust made the sex so much more enjoyable.

Liliana tried to focus on Max's reactions to her movements, but she couldn't ignore the sensations herself. The two of them were reaching the crescendo when Max lost control and thrust into her repeatedly, sending them spiralling together. Their lips crashed together as they enjoyed each other fully. Slowing down to revel in the moment, they softly kissed each other. Liliana's hands now back in Max's hair while his hands dropped to her waist, pulling her closer as they embraced.

"Feel better?" Max asked. The grin had returned.

"Much," Liliana laughed. Her boyfriend had an interesting method of distracting her from her job.

*

She wished she could feel that level of trust again. That level of intimacy. Even if she were standing right in front of Max, she didn't think they could connect on that level anymore. Their reunion was sure to be complicated. Part of Liliana wanted to avoid the confrontation, but she knew it had to happen if their relationship stood any chance.

Chapter Nineteen

"You know how to do your job, Tim. You've been in this field as long as I have," Rose groaned. He wouldn't leave her alone. Acting like he was an intern on his first day.

"I was told to talk to you about settling in here," Tim said. "And that's exactly what I plan to do." He was being his usual smug self, and Rose hated it.

"Sit down at a computer and write. Research. Find a story to tell." Rose dumbed his job down for him as much as possible, trying to make him sit down and leave her alone.

"What system do you use?" Tim asked.

"Google," she replied sarcastically.

"You know what I meant, Rosie." Tim raised his eyebrow. "Where do you store your work? How do I get onto the server?"

"You should have got your login details via email," she replied.

That seemed to have finally shut him up. He was engrossed in his computer. Rose took the opportunity to run off for a coffee while his back was turned. She hurried into the café they camped out-side of still.

"Hi, Carl," she greeted the owner, glad to see he had escaped the big fight with barely a cut or bruise on his colossal frame.

"How are you, dear?" he asked as he started mak-ing her usual order. "I hear they've replaced Liliana already. Hard to believe." He was one of the few people in the city who believed that Liliana was completely innocent in all of it. He hated how she was being treated.

"Well, I'll be ready to shoot the replacement any day now," Rose replied.

"How long have you been working with them?" Carl asked, confused.

"A couple of hours," she answered, a malicious grin forming on her face. Carl chuckled in response.

"That bad, huh?"

"You have no idea. The guy is good at what he does, to be fair. But he's a right jackass about it all." Rose enjoyed complaining to Carl. He was always happy to listen.

"Ah, one of those types. What's his name?"

"Tim Westfield," she replied.

"You talking about me, Rosie?" Tim asked, walking through the café door just at the wrong moment.

"Oh god," she groaned, unable to escape him once

again.

"This is a cute little shop." He stopped to look around, completely ignoring Carl for the moment.

"Cute?" Carl asked. He was quite defensive of his coffee shop. God knows what he would have done if they destroyed it in the fight.

Tim just continued to look around, taking in the artwork on the walls. Carl was proud to show off a collection from some local artists. True, the pieces weren't to everyone's taste, but it added character to the shop. Gave people something to talk about.

"Coffee, please. Black, two sugars," Tim shot across to Carl without even making eye contact.

"Come again?" Carl wasn't one to back down against rude customers.

"Try that again, but with some manners," Rose added on. She would not let anyone mistreat Carl.

Tim just stared at Rose for a moment, as if he could make her apologise to him. Then he sighed and turned to Carl.

"Could I have a coffee, please? Black with two sugars?" Tim asked in an overly sweet tone, obviously trying to placate Rose. The annoyed look on Carl's face did not put him off. Carl may not be hulkingly tall, but something about him usually puts people off a confrontation.

"Sure. That'll be five dollars," Carl replied, not breaking eye contact. Tim just pulled some cash out of his pocket and threw it down on the counter. Rose stepped back, not wanting to impede Carl kicking Tim's ass. Hell, she wanted a good place to watch.

Carl looked down at the cash lying on his counter and back up at Tim, waiting for him to pick it up. He wasn't blinking. He looked like he was mentally preparing for a fight. They stared each other down for a minute or two before Tim finally broke. He picked up the cash, counted out five dollars, and handed it over to Carl properly.

"That wasn't so hard, now was it?" Carl said, rubbing it in a little. He turned to make the coffee and deposit the cash in the till. Not a moment later, Tim's coffee sat on the counter and pushed slightly towards Tim. He looked suspiciously calm and collected, despite the confrontation.

"So, Rose, how is our Liliana doing? Have you heard from her?" Carl returned to their previous conversation as if Tim had never interrupted them.

"She's doing okay. Job hunting mainly. She checks in every so often," Rose replied, happy to ignore Tim as well.

"Good, good. You let her know I'm thinking of her next time you speak."

"I will. Thank you, Carl." Rose left him to his other customers with a smile. Tim walked out behind her, clutching his coffee tightly.

"What an asshole," he remarked as soon as they were out of earshot.

"Coming from you?" Rose replied before she could stop herself.

"Excuse me?" Tim asked, somehow surprised by her reply.

"Carl is the nicest person I've ever met. It's your own fault you pissed him off."

Tim looked like he wanted to respond, but he seemed torn, unsure of what to say.

"Yeah, that's what I thought," Rose replied to his silence before walking back to her desk.

*

A couple of hours later, Tim distracted himself with networking with the other reporters. Everyone else around Rose seemed to be happy to welcome him into the fold. He was the poster boy for charming to the rest of the deconstructed office.

Rose was struggling to get on with her work. Her co-workers kept coming up to her to praise Tim and tell her how lucky she was to be working closely with him. She prayed to any god that was listening that they just meant them sitting next to each other. If Tanya had paired them up on the job, she wouldn't be able to stop arguing the point with Tanya. Although, knowing her luck, that would be exactly what was about to happen.

She hadn't actually seen Tim do any work; he

had barely stayed still since he arrived that morning. He had taken Tanya to lunch nearby, happy to brownnose his way into her bitter heart. It seemed like she would be endlessly listening to Tim's praises when an email pinged on her laptop. They needed her to cover another speech a couple of streets away. The Mayor, again. He was finally going to address the fight, it seemed.

She left the makeshift office as soon as she could shut down her computer, remembering to grab her cameras as she went. The speech was close enough to warrant a walk rather than trying to flag down a taxi at this time of day.

Rose walked down the street, a few remnants of the fight visible still, wishing the fresh, Tim-free air would help clear her mind. How she wished she could rant to Liliana right now. She knew she would be on her side with Tim. They spent many evenings complaining about him in the past couple of years. What started out as simple journalistic rivalry had soon turned into a genuinely terrible professional relationship. The guy just creeped them out, plain and simple.

Now Rose would not be able to escape him. She was being forced to work with him because Tanya couldn't stand a little bad press by keeping Liliana on. Although, if Liliana was planning something to do with Max, she probably needed all the spare time she could get.

Rose knew Liliana had to lie to her. Telling her she was finished with Max, done with men altogether. They loved each other too much for her to move on that quickly. Even if Liliana had thrown Max aside, she would be heartbroken for weeks, if not months, afterwards. Thankfully, it seemed the rest of the world bought into the lie. They didn't know Liliana like Rose did. And she would keep the secret, she would protect her best friend. No matter what.

Rose rounded the last corner to see the press stand set up outside City Hall. The Mayor was staying on home turf this time, giving himself an easy exit. Smart. No specific press area this time. It was to be a free-for-all kind of speech. That always made her job more interesting. She nudged her way through the gathering crowd to find herself a suitable spot to capture the speech.

It appeared to be cosmic timing that, as soon as her gear was set up and she couldn't run away, Tim appeared out of nowhere.

"You ran off rather quickly," Tim said. He dropped his bag to his feet and pulled out his reporter's kit, ready for the speech.

"Don't tell me. Tanya's paired us up?" Rose groaned. She would not escape him, after all.

"Well, you were the only photographer not paired with anyone." As annoying as Tim was, he was right. It would have made sense to put them together. Rose was now half wishing she followed Liliana and walked out of the company.

"Let's get on with it, then. I'm set up and ready to go." Rose resigned herself to working with Tim one-on-one. She had lucked out previously, working with her best friend for years. Her luck was due to turn against her, and it had chosen Tim as her punishment.

*

The speech wasn't as interesting as the previous one. No one heckling from the crowd this time. It was your typical politician's speech after a disaster like the fight.

"We're keeping the injured and their families in our thoughts and prayers."

"We can only be thankful that Sentinel has apprehended the cause of all this trauma and damage."

"This only shows that the Taskforce launched just a couple of days ago is very much needed in this city."

Tim was eating up the speech. He loved what the Mayor was giving him. Rose, however, just stood there, seeing right through the Mayor. She could see what worried Max. He was ready to hand over so much power to those already over-powered by sheer coincidence.

But it trapped her. She couldn't talk about it publicly. She was sure Sentinel was still listening in, somehow. She had to continue her life as if nothing had changed. As if she still adored the man who saved her life. If only Sentinel was that straightforward. Why couldn't he just be the good guy?

A cloud of confusion had followed Rose since that moment in Liliana's hospital room. Since Max's letter. She didn't want to believe it, but she had to. Rose worked with the news every day, faced with unearthing the truth at every turn. She couldn't ignore it now.

She wanted to help Liliana, if only to escape the gaze of Sentinel, but she did not know how. She didn't have the benefit of a rich boyfriend to lean on during all of this. Not that she wanted a rich boyfriend, of course. But Liliana had that working to her advantage. No. She was on her own in this.

"Are you okay, Rose?" a voice asked, working through the cloudiness of Rose's mind, bringing her back to the present.

"Sorry?" Rose asked.

"I asked if you are okay?" Tim replied. "You have an odd look on your face. What's going on?"

For once, he actually seemed sincere in his questioning. If Tim hadn't been such an ass in the past, Rose might actually believe he was a nice guy.

"I'm fine. Just got a lot on my mind," Rose replied as she gathered up her camera equipment.

"If you're sure," Tim said.

"I'm sure. Let's just get back to the office," Rose said.

Tim picked up his bags and started walking along with Rose. She didn't know if she should start up a conversation with Tim or not. They weren't friendly by any measure, but the silence was quickly becoming awkward.

"So, how are you finding working for our paper? Different from your last place?" Rose asked, breaking the uncomfortable silence.

"Well, the location is certainly different," he replied sarcastically.

"Well, yeah, of course it is."

"But aside from that, it's nice to change it up. I didn't really have much of a chance of career progression in my last place. The editor was young and full of ideas. No chance I could steal their job soon."

"Tanya's not exactly old," Rose replied, confused. Why switch one immovable editor for another?

"No, but she might move on up soon. You know she has high ambitions," Tim replied. Rose had to agree, that made sense.

"What makes you think you'll get her job if she moves on?" Rose asked. "You're the newbie, despite your previous experience. You have a lot of competition here."

"A chance is better than nothing. Besides, I like my

chances." There was his smug attitude once again. Just when Rose was thinking he might have a pleasant side.

"What about you? Any thoughts on a promotion soon?" Tim asked, bumping her shoulder as they walked. A little too friendly for her liking.

"Not so much a promotion. More of a sideways step. I've been considering going freelance," Rose replied, not sure why she was opening up to Tim already.

"Freelance? A bit risky, isn't it?" Tim asked.

"Maybe, but there're more opportunities when you're your own boss," she replied.

"True. I don't think it's for me, though. I enjoy having a base of operations, one solid role. Maybe a few people reporting to me." Tim looked wistful as he described his ideal position.

"You'll be reporting the same stories over and over, though. I'd like more variety myself, even if it comes with the risk of unemployment for a time," Rose argued.

"What's wrong with stability? Security? Makes more sense to me," Tim replied. It was clearer than ever that the two were starkly different in how they operated. "Anyway, no point disagreeing on this, it's all theoretical at this point, isn't it?"

"I suppose," Rose said.

Together, they rounded the last corner before their

makeshift office appeared. Rose looked up at their building, half expecting to see Sentinel appear, helping the repairs whilst listening in on her conversations. But he was nowhere to be seen. She was sure he was somewhere close, though, keeping tabs on her.

"Fancy getting a drink after work?" Tim asked, out of the blue.

"It's Wednesday, Tim," she replied.

"So?" he asked.

"No, thanks," Rose answered.

"Why not? I thought we were getting on pretty well then." He stepped in front of her to look into her eyes as he spoke.

"I'm not much of a drinker." Rose tried to sidestep Tim to get back to her desk.

"I'm fun on a date, trust me, you'll enjoy it." Tim stepped back in front of her. He wasn't going to take no for an answer.

"I said no, thank you," Rose replied. As a reply, Tim stepped closer and placed his hand on her arm.

"Are you sure I can't tempt you?" He dropped his voice down low, a small smile trying to encourage her to say yes. Rose had enough. She shrugged his hand off her arm and shouted.

"Tim. I said no. I don't want to go on a date with you." Tim moved back slightly, a frown taking the place of his smile a moment ago. "Do you know why?"

"Why?" Tim asked begrudgingly.

"I'm gay, Tim." Rose saw the understanding flash across his face.

"Oh."

"Yeah, 'oh'," Rose said. "I'm not sure how you missed it. I'm quite open about my love of the ladies."

Tim at least had the decency to look embarrassed by his actions, just not apologetic. Rose finally stepped around him and walked towards her desk. She noticed a few of their colleagues were listening in on Tim's failed romance attempt. He turned around to see the look of amusement on their faces, his cheeks flushing pink in embarrassment.

She wouldn't have made him feel so bad about it if he hadn't been so pushy. Maybe this embarrassment would make him think twice in the future. Then again, probably not. If he was that pushy with someone he doesn't really get along with, what was he like with friendly girls? She hated to think.

Chapter Twenty

Liliana received yet another rejection email, the fourth that morning. Confusingly, she felt both relieved and annoyed at the email. She made a quick post on her social media accounts, bemoaning her lack of job opportunities because of Max. She shared some posts about the relief effort in the city and replied to some comments from acquaintances. She found it boring, but she needed to keep up appearances.

Her phone beeped at her, bringing her out of the boredom of job hunting. It was a message from Rose.

Rose: *You'll never guess what just happened!*

Liliana: *What?!*

Rose: *Tim just asked me out! Can you believe him?*

Liliana: *No way! Doesn't he know he doesn't have the right parts?*

Rose: *I pointed that out to him.*

Liliana: *LOL*

Rose: *He didn't help himself by doing it right in front*

of the entire office.

Liliana: *Wish I had been there to see that.*

Rose: *It was pretty fun. Wouldn't have been so bad if he wasn't so pushy when I said no the first time.*

Liliana: *Ugh. He's one of those? I shouldn't be surprised.*

Rose: *The look on his face, though! Should make him think twice the next time, I hope.*

Liliana: *Brilliant!*

She couldn't help but chuckle at the thought of Tim being shot down by a lesbian. How he didn't know already she couldn't figure out. It was fairly obvious to anyone with eyes.

"What's so funny?" Yates asked as they came into the room. They had pencil smudges all over their hands. Yates had been hard at work, designing Liliana's new suit. She envied their artistic abilities. Liliana filled Yates in on the news.

"Mr Victor mentioned Mr Westfield to me a couple of times. He sounds like an unpleasant man," Yates replied.

"That's putting it nicely, Yates," Liliana said.

"Ah," Yates replied, grabbing a cloth to clean the smudges off their hands. "Coffee?" they asked.

"Please," Liliana answered.

Liliana stood and followed Yates into the kitchen. She needed to stretch her legs a little. While Yates made the coffee using a special method that made the coffee taste one hundred percent better than when she made it herself, Liliana dug out some biscuits from the snack cupboard.

"I feel like I need to be doing something more while we prepare," Liliana blurted out.

"What do you mean?" Yates asked, their brow furrowed in confusion.

"Like, I know we're training and planning for the mission, and that's very important. I know that," Liliana started. "But all this fake job hunting has got me thinking. Maybe I should do something else as well, something to help the city. Try to make them realise why Max's point is so important. But maybe something more subtle than what Max did." She wasn't sure if there was a happy middle ground. Maybe she was spouting nonsense.

"You want to make people understand the Supers aren't all that great, but you don't want to start a fight with them?" Yates asked, clarifying Liliana's ramblings.

"Yeah, exactly. Is that even possible?" Liliana replied, unsure if what she was asking was even possible.

"Well, you could use your journalistic training," Yates replied. "Maybe do some research into the Supers and post it online."

"What, like a blog?" Liliana asked.

"Yeah. Make it available for the city, let them draw their own conclusions. Give them a different point of view to what they're being force-fed by the media." Yates handed Liliana her coffee as she explained her point.

"Do you think people will even bother with it?" Liliana heard of new blogs every day, soon fizzling out to nothing within a month.

"Why don't you use Mr Victor's servers and algorithms to boost it? You could push it out to everyone in the city."

"You have something like that here?" Liliana wasn't sure if that sounded completely legal.

"It's proprietary technology, not something Mr Victor made public knowledge," Yates explained. "You can't use it to hack into people's technology, but you can use it to send them information."

"Okay. So, ignoring the legality issue for a moment, I could use this system to give the public information that's being suppressed about the Supers." Liliana liked that idea the more she thought about it. "That's something I can do. It might even help Max's case. Get some public opinion behind him instead of Sentinel."

"That might be a bit of a stretch. Everyone's saying that Mr Victor was the aggressor in the fight. That he's blamed for all the damage and the deaths," Yates argued. "It'll take some hard evidence to prove to them he isn't to blame, not just some articles on the internet."

"That's true, I suppose. But it's a start," Liliana counterpointed.

"Exactly. It's better than nothing. If you can weaken the public's love of the Supers, it might halt this new Taskforce in its tracks," Yates said.

Liliana thanked Yates for their advice and took her computer down the winding hallways to find the broadcasting room. Yates pointed her in the right direction. She felt like she had a purpose now, outside of training for the mission. She could distract herself with this now in her down time. She didn't like to sit with her thoughts for very long, they weren't very pleasant.

She turned from corridor to corridor, trying to remember Yates's instructions. She was still amazed at the depth of Max's secret base. How long had he spent building it, tunnelling down into the hillside? The entire mound must be hollow by this point. She couldn't help but be impressed every time she found a new section to explore, more rooms she didn't know existed. How Max and Yates got around without a map, she did not know.

Several minutes later, she finally found the room she was looking for. It wasn't very large. A wall filled with technology, a couple of desks and chairs, and a couple of lamps lighting up the room. That was all. Liliana took it all in. She didn't understand how all the technology worked, but Yates said it should be pretty straightforward to use. Just plug in her computer and switch the wall of tech on.

She sat before the wall, flipped her laptop open and on, plugged it in to the nearest port and hit the clearly labelled on/off switch above her. Her laptop screen was mirrored and expanded on several screens around her, giving her more space to work with. She pulled up a browser window and got to work building her new website.

It was important to remain anonymous with this website. She had to make sure it didn't lead back to her at all. Otherwise, all the work she'd been putting into her public profile would be dead in the water. She could hear the tech surrounding her whirl to life as she began her work.

*

Several hours later, Liliana emerged from the broadcasting room, her eyes aching from the work she put them through. The website was complete, an introductory piece already live for everyone to read. She needed to dig back through Max's research on the Supers and put the results into articles for the public to read. As she made her way back through the complex, she stopped in the research room to grab a handful of files to work on later that night.

She entered the main living space to see Yates pouring over the mission plans on the coffee table next to the sofa.

"Needed a change of scenery?" Liliana asked, for once happy that she sneaked up on Yates rather than the other way around. She was rewarded by seeing Yates jump a little as they heard her voice.

"Yes. I was getting too cooped up in that room. I hope you don't mind me taking over the table," Yates replied, seeing the files Liliana was carrying.

"No, that's fine. Everything looking okay with the plans?" Liliana dropped her files down on the side table next to the sofa and sat across from Yates, glancing over the mission plans.

"I believe so. We have the guards' rota figured out now, so they are easy to work around. The only wild card is Sentinel. He still visits the prison occasionally. I can't seem to get a handle on his pattern, though. I think it might be worth planning the mission for a time we know he will be unavailable," Yates reeled off. Liliana nodded along with their ideas.

"Isn't he scheduled to appear on panel shows at the end of the month?" Liliana asked. Sentinel liked the publicity of TV. He often made appearances to boost his rating amongst the public.

"Yes!" Yates approved, pulling a sheet of paper from the bottom of a pile close by. "He's going to be live on air for several hours, two weeks on Friday. Perfect."

"Two weeks," Liliana repeated, suddenly feeling the weight of the task at hand. Her chest tightened as the anxiety settled in.

"I'll make sure you're ready for it. Don't worry," Yates said, noticing Liliana panicking. "With all the planning we've put in and the tech at our disposal, this'll be a walk in the park." Yates smiled at Liliana, calming her nerves.

"Okay. I trust you," Liliana said, and she meant it. She could see why Max trusted Yates so much. They really were a wonderful person. "So, what else needs planning?"

Together they spent the evening ironing out the rest of the plans for the prison break. It was daunting, but Liliana was finally feeling prepared for it.

Chapter Twenty-One

Liliana woke from what must have been the best night's sleep she'd had since the fight. They had the plan nailed down to a T and she was well on her way to being physically prepared for it. Sentinel would not be an issue. It was just any rogue guards who might cross their path on the day she had to worry about. She could do it. At least, that's what she kept repeating to herself. She could do it. She was prepared. It had become a little mantra she said to herself multiple times a day.

Her little room in the complex was slowly feeling like home. She hadn't filled it with belongings, but she felt safe here. That was the chief thing she loved about this complex. No one else knew it existed. No intruding police officers or superheroes. No one listening in. Just her and Yates. She and Yates against the world it felt like sometimes.

She had a day of training and research set out for her. First her body was going to be beaten up, then her mind. It was exhausting yet rewarding work. After washing up and dressing in loose clothing, Liliana trekked down to the kitchen in search of breakfast.

After making herself toast and coffee, she walked into the living area to see Yates standing in front of the TV, a deep frown marking their face.

"Why so grumpy this early in the morning?" Liliana asked, trying to lighten the mood. Yates just pointed at the screen.

"...known for the partial destruction of the city earlier this month. The Taskforce have made the decision to move Max Victor to a more secure prison complex. This is in response to news of a potential prison break being planned."

"*Ay, carajo!*" Liliana half shouted as she watched the news. "How did they find out? Are we in danger, Yates?"

"No. They do not know who is planning the prison break. Only that it's a possibility." Yates switched off the TV as they looped the footage of the fight.

"But what does this mean? Is Max stuck?" Liliana asked, unsure of her next steps.

"They are moving him at the end of the week. Moving him across the country to the most secure prison they can." Yates slumped down onto the sofa as they spoke. "If we don't free Mr Victor before they move him, we won't stand a chance. Even Mr Victor doesn't have the resources to break out of there."

"So, we don't have two weeks to prepare?" Liliana

asked, sure she didn't like the answer that was coming.

"We have two days," Yates confirmed Liliana's fears. Two days was not enough time. Not nearly enough time.

She felt the panic from the previous night return, her happy calm a long-lost memory. At least she had one good night's sleep before this news came crashing down on them. Two days to prepare. Two days to learn how to fight properly. Two days to finish her research. Two days for Yates to finish her suit, otherwise she would be badly exposed. Two days. Crap.

"We need to get to work," Yates said, standing back up, their eyes darting from side to side, trying to catch up with their thoughts. "Go start your training routine. Get through as much as you can alone for now. I'll come down and spar once I'm finished."

Liliana nodded. As odd as it was to get orders from Yates, she couldn't help but to defer to their authority in this situation. She drained the end of her coffee and ate her toast as she made her way down to the gym, suddenly glad she was dressed in loose clothing already. She had run through the training routine enough times to have it memorised by now, but she was determined to push herself further this time. Hitting harder, running faster. She needed to be ready.

As she trained, she imagined she was fighting Sentinel. Only, she actually stood a chance at winning. Not terribly realistic, but it was mildly cathartic. Punching bags, treadmills, and weight lifting filled her morning. Yates was busy doing whatever they were doing, so Liliana ran through more drills than she originally planned while she waited. Being stationary felt wrong right now, no matter how tired her body was getting.

"Stop. You're pushing yourself too much. You'll cause damage soon enough." Yates's voice pulled her out of her workout, breaking her focus. She dropped the weights to the floor, narrowly missing her feet.

"But I need to prepare," Liliana disagreed.

"Not like this. This is counterproductive," Yates admonished her. "We'll spar later on. Cool off and follow me." Liliana grabbed her water bottle from the side, downed half of it, and poured the rest over her face. Messy but helpful. She'd worked up quite the sweat during her workout.

She grabbed a towel and followed Yates back upstairs into the living space, then through the corridors, back to the design room. Liliana figured Yates had locked themselves away for the entire morning working on a project. Liliana was almost excited to see what Yates had to show her.

Liliana mopped up the sweat running down her face and neck as she walked into the design room.

She was briefly lost for words once she saw the suit standing in the middle of the room. It was dark, slim-fitting, and gorgeous. It appeared to cover every inch of skin on the mannequin underneath it, showing how protective it was. As promised, there was no cape, but there was a half skirt that ran around the back of her waist.

Liliana walked slowly around the suit, taking in every detail. There were some chunkier sections to it which Liliana couldn't figure out around the lower arms and the hips. Were they compartments? Extra padding? She couldn't decide.

She gingerly held out a hand to feel the material. It was tough, like leather, but there was an element to it she couldn't put her finger on. There were harder sections along the shoulders, on the outside of the arms and legs. They were definitely for extra protection.

There was just one thing she couldn't figure out.

"How do I put it on?" Liliana asked Yates, who was standing back by the door, watching her reaction to the suit. Yates pulled a small controller out of their pocket and pressed a button. A seam appeared, running from head to toe of the suit, opening it up mechanically, giving her space to step in. It surprised Liliana to see there was no mannequin inside the suit holding it up, they simply made it strong enough to stand on its own. Liliana wondered just how much armour Yates added to it.

"Okay. That's amazing," Liliana was in awe of Yates's work. Holding back from bouncing on her heels, she turned to face Yates and stepped back into the suit. It closed around her, fitting her perfectly. She felt the suit lock around her legs, then her waist, before sealing over her head. It was dark briefly, but before the claustrophobia could kick in a light appeared in front of her. It was a view screen, showing the surrounding room with information overlaying the images. The suit scanned the room, reporting back no danger, but it did scan Yates to give her their vitals.

"This is amazing. Yates, you are brilliant!" Liliana said, taken aback by the nondescript voice that came out of the suit. It altered her voice to protect her identity. This suit just kept getting cooler.

"I'm glad you like it," Yates replied. They moved over to the design table and pulled up a set of graphs Liliana hadn't seen before. "The suit is reporting back okay. The scans are working, no bugs are being reported so far."

"You're getting readings from the suit?" Liliana asked.

"Yes. After the problems with Mr Victor's fight with Sentinel I thought it best to be able to access the suit," Yates explained.

"I suppose that's fair enough," Liliana agreed.

"I've included a comms system. It has a pretty decent range, so we will keep in contact. As well as with anyone else on the system in the future," Yates said.

Liliana heard a blip to her left as Yates pressed the comms button to show Liliana. She moved her hand up to the helmet to feel it. She found it weird, moving the arm of the suit so easily. She expected it to be heavy and clunky. Instead, it felt like she was just wearing a thick coat.

She moved around, getting a good feel for the suit. Her feet felt heavy as she walked, but it wasn't too bad. She walked around the design room, using the viewscreen to look around as she went. She walked back to Yates as she fiddled with the chunkier sections on her forearms.

"Don't fiddle too much there." Yates held out their hands to stop her from poking around.

"Why, what are they?" Liliana asked, pausing in her tracks.

"Weapons," Yates answered. "I fitted several options, as a last resort kind of option. We shouldn't need them for the mission. I hope we won't." Yates walked forward to show Liliana what to do with the weapons.

Yates held Liliana's arm and pointed to different sections on her forearms. As Liliana focused on each section, the option to view and use the weapons appeared on her viewscreen. She didn't feel too comfortable having this kind of firepower strapped to her, but she tried to remain calm to be sure she didn't accidentally set something off. She had guns, small explosives, and percussive weapons available for her to use.

"This is all suddenly feeling very real and a little overwhelming." Liliana took a couple of deep breaths as she took in everything that was happening.

She didn't have long to calm herself down. An alert flashed up on the viewscreen at the same time as it showed up on Yates's tech. "INTRUDER" flashed across her line of sight before bringing up a live video of someone walking into the garage below them. Liliana and Yates barely glanced at each other before they raced out of the room and down to confront the unknown man.

Liliana didn't have long to think, long enough to realise that anyone who had found the complex was a threat. Only three people knew about it, and the only one not present was locked away. So she reacted. She jumped into the garage from above and tackled the intruder, her new suit allowing her to reach the man before Yates. Without thinking, she put her recent training to use and pinned the man down to the floor underneath her, restraining his arms behind him so he couldn't move. He didn't make a sound of pain, only shock at the attack.

Yates threw Liliana a pair of handcuffs to secure the intruder, which she caught with her uncovered hand. They locked around the man's wrists, lighting up as they did so. They weren't your usual lock-and-key handcuffs. They required the fingerprints of the person locking them to open. Once the man was secure, Liliana pulled him to his knees so they could question him together.

Liliana felt shock shoot through her body as she looked at the man. She paused, her hands still on his shoulders as he steadied himself on the garage floor. After a moment she stepped back and, before Yates could speak, she opened the suit up around her head only to get a better look at him.

"Johnathon?" she asked, wondering how a dead man had found his way into their super-secret complex.

Chapter Twenty-Two

"You know this man?" Yates asked, staring Johnathon down.

"I used to work with him," Liliana replied. "I was told he died when the office building was attacked." She couldn't believe what she was seeing. Johnathon, alive and kneeling in front of her.

"How are you alive? I saw you go inside the building right before it was destroyed," she asked.

"I was inside," Johnathon replied, his voice showing his surprise and a bit of fear.

"So, how did you survive? It reduced our entire floor to rubble," she asked, needing to know the answer.

"I escaped with the others. We got out before they hit the floor." His answer didn't quite ring true.

"But Tanya knew who got out and who didn't. She said you didn't make it," Liliana replied. Johnathon was lying, they all knew it.

"She must have missed me. I'm alive, obviously," Johnathon lied again.

"Don't move," Yates ordered, stepping back to the other side of the room. Liliana followed them.

"How is this possible?" Liliana whispered to Yates.

"There is the possibility they simply missed him in the aftermath," Yates said. "But why wouldn't he have come forward by now?"

"Exactly. It was his first day on the job, he was so excited to work for the paper. Why would he let people believe he was dead?" Liliana couldn't wrap her head around what was happening.

"Put your helmet back up, use the suit to scan him," Yates suggested.

Liliana turned back to face Johnathon as she activated the helmet again. The suit was very intuitive. It scanned him almost immediately. Slightly elevated heart rate, to be expected in this situation. No signs of any injuries, surprising given he was in the building when the fight started. In fact, no signs of any injuries, ever. No scars, no previously broken bones, no antibodies for any major illnesses aside from the vaccines he would have received growing up. Johnathon had somehow got through life with no health complications.

Liliana thought back to the day of the fight, their quick trip for coffee. Johnathon gulped down a scoldingly hot coffee with no consequence. He didn't feel the heat. Liliana focused the scan on his mouth for a moment. Her hunch paid off, no signs of a recent burn. What was going on here? She deactivated the helmet and turned back to Yates.

"He's perfectly fine. No injuries."

"Okay. So he got lucky during the fight," Yates said, not grasping Liliana's point.

"No. I mean, no injuries, ever." Yates looked at Liliana, confused. "There should at least be a burn from the scolding coffee he gulped down in front of me right before the fight. He has no signs of ever being injured or ill."

Yates's jaw dropped a little as comprehension showed in their eyes. They looked back at Johnathon with a curious look in their eyes.

"Do you know what this means?" Yates asked.

"That he's a medical marvel?" Liliana replied.

"No," Yates said. They stormed back towards Johnathon, a determined look on their face. Liliana hurried after them, wondering what Yates had planned.

"How long have you known?" Yates asked Johnathon.

"Known what?" He looked uneasy at the sudden questioning.

"That you're invulnerable," Yates replied.

Liliana gasped as it all made sense to her. He wasn't a medical marvel; he couldn't get injured or sick. Nothing would affect him.

"He's a Super?" Liliana asked, trying to get it all

straight in her mind. "You weren't lucky to escape. You got caught up in the building's destruction. It just didn't hurt you."

Johnathon hung his head in resignation. His secret was out.

"Yes," he admitted. "But I'm not a Super. I'm no hero. I'm a freak."

"What?" Liliana was taken aback by his words. "You're not a freak. You have the gene."

Liliana could see this was something Johnathon had struggled with for some time now. She understood why he had never made his ability public.

"How did you find this place?" Yates brought them back 'round to the major concern. Was their secret hideout no longer a secret?

"I noticed Liliana had been disappearing somewhere. I've been trying to find you," Johnathon said to them both. "I know you're up to something. I saw you were together. Why would you be with Max Victor's bodyguard if you truly believed him to be the villain?"

"Fair point," Liliana replied. "But how did you find the base? We had no vehicles following us, we're out in the middle of nowhere."

"I always enjoyed hiking." Johnathon shrugged his shoulders as he explained, like hiking through the local wilderness for days was nothing to him.

"Why did you want to find Ms Masters?" Yates

asked, taking everything in.

"Because I knew that if she believed Max Victor to be the innocent party, I could help her," Johnathon replied. "I saw the fight, up close."

"You saw Max?" Liliana asked, getting more curious every minute.

"I saw them both. I saw the shot that destroyed the building," Johnathon replied. "Max was trying to stop Sentinel from getting to the office building. He was trying to protect it. Protect you."

"Sentinel was trying to get to me?" Liliana asked, not sure she wanted to know the answer.

"He was trying to kill you," Johnathon revealed. "That energy blast? He aimed it at your desk."

Liliana stumbled backwards towards the nearest seat, collapsing into it as she realised she had a target on her back.

"What did I do to deserve this?" Liliana asked.

"Actually, it's more of a question of who did you do?" Johnathon joked, not realising that this wasn't really the time for humour. Liliana shot a glare at him which shut him up for the moment.

"This is because of my relationship with Max?" she questioned. "So, Sentinel must have known it was Max he was fighting to start with. That's why Max was trying to find out who Sentinel is, he wanted to protect me."

Liliana lent forward and ran her hands through her dark hair, running these revelations through her mind.

"Until that fight, I thought the Supers were doing the right thing. That they had the public's interests at heart. But if Sentinel could try to kill you like that, what does it mean for the city when they give him autonomy?" Johnathon explained. "That's when I knew I had to do something. To stop Sentinel, and anyone like him."

"So you want to become a Super like them? Or a villain I suppose, if you're planning to oppose them," Liliana said.

"Why must there be only two options? Good or evil, there's really no binary if you really think about it," Johnathon replied, making a good point.

"You're telling me," Yates replied under their breath. They seemed to warm up to Johnathon. He was spouting all the right ideas and he wasn't fighting back against them. Yates and Liliana had only two options before them. Trust Johnathon and set him free, hoping he wouldn't rat them out to Sentinel, or lock him up until the mission was complete.

"So, what should we do with him?" Yates asked Liliana.

"I think we can trust him. If he were working with Sentinel, we wouldn't be sitting here talking. We would already be captured or killed. Sentinel isn't one to wait around," Liliana rationalised. Yates nodded, agreeing with her assessment. Liliana walked over to Johnathon, deactivated the gloves on her suit and unlocked the handcuffs, releasing him.

"So, what do we do now?" Johnathon stood, rubbing his wrists to get rid of the pressure marks of the handcuffs.

"We prepare. We have two days to get Max out of prison," Liliana said, looking between Johnathon and Yates. With a Super on their side, they might actually stand a chance at pulling this off.

*

Rose was stressing out. She hadn't heard a word from Liliana since the news broke of Max's prison move. She knew Liliana was planning something. It frustrated her that she couldn't be told what it was. She wanted to help, somehow. She even suspected that the articles being pushed out on her tech were from her. They had appeared all over the city, on almost every device. The office was buzzing with them. The controversial opinions had been getting people talking. Most dismissed the articles for pure nonsense, but some looked to be swayed by the new information.

She shot off another text to Liliana, hoping she might get a reply sometime soon. She was home, trying not to pay attention to the coverage of Max's prison move on the television, her dinner left half eaten on her kitchen counter next to the mostly empty bottle of wine. True, she hadn't started it that day, but she was drinking more than she probably should.

She paced up and down her living room, glancing at the television occasionally, gulping down her wine. She checked her phone every ten seconds, waiting for a response that was probably not coming that night. A knock at the door jolted her out of her routine.

"Who on earth? It's eleven o'clock at night!" She opened her door, expecting to shout at whoever was knocking this late, only to see an empty corridor. "What the?" She stuck her head out to look up and down the hall, no one in sight. She locked the door and turned back around. Only to scream.

"Hello, my dear," Sentinel said as he hovered in her living room.

"What the— How did—" Rose spluttered, trying to understand why Sentinel was hovering in her living room. "What are you doing in my house?" She finally got the words out.

"I knocked," Sentinel replied, completely missing how messed up his actions were.

"That's not really my point," Rose said, still not understanding what was going on.

"I wanted to talk to you, away from the cameras this time, if you don't mind," Sentinel said, ignoring the blatant invasion of privacy he had just committed.

"About what?" Rose replied, unsure of how to act.

"Ms Masters and her acquaintances," Sentinel replied. "Have you heard from her since we last spoke?"

"Only the drinks we had the other night, although I'm sure you know about that already," Rose replied, deciding partial honesty might hide her suspicions.

"Of course. But nothing since?" Sentinel asked. "You see, we are concerned about her welfare."

"Her welfare? She's fine. She's just trying to distance herself from all of this, that's all," Rose replied.

"So as far as you know, she hasn't fallen in with the wrong sort?" Sentinel hovered closer to Rose, staring straight at her, waiting for her to lie.

"No. Max fooled her, but she knows better now. She's keeping clear of that whole situation," Rose replied, hoping against hope that Sentinel believed her.

"Very well," Sentinel said calmly. He moved back and took a smooth glance around the apartment. "What a lovely home you have." A simple statement that sent chills down Rose's spine. Her discomfort was reaching a discerning level.

"Thank you." Rose felt like she had to reply kindly.

All she wanted was for Sentinel to leave. Although, did she feel safe in her own home anymore? Is this what Liliana felt like?

Sentinel finished looking around her home, although he took his time about it. "I'll be going now. Please let me know if you hear from Ms Masters. I would very much like to speak to her." He hovered back towards Rose, arm outstretched, handing her a business card. His hands were remarkably well looked after, surprising for a man in his line of work. Not a chipped nail to be seen. There might have even been a glint of clear polish. A manicure?

Why does a superhero need a business card? That didn't seem right to Rose. She looked the card over. All it had was a number to call. No other details. She flipped it over to be sure. She looked back at Sentinel not a moment later to see an empty apartment. He had disappeared as quickly as he appeared.

Chapter Twenty-Three

Liliana split her time between the gym and the broadcasting room, leaving a few hours in between for sleep and food. She was trying to fit two weeks' worth of work into two days and finding it impossible.

She was sore, sorer than after Max and Sentinel's big fight. Yates had really been putting her through the ringer. But her mind was buzzing. The thrill of broadcasting an anonymous blog, showing the city the truth, had given her such a high. While the training was useful, the blog had given Liliana a genuine sense of purpose. She could imagine the people spread throughout the city reading her work, understanding the truth of the Super situation.

While she couldn't see how many people were believing her, she could see the statistics of the people reading her work. The numbers were climbing by the hour. She had been pumping out information as quickly as she could, putting her years of journalism training to use.

Yates had pulled Johnathon into the design room.

They were planning a suit for him as well. Although he didn't really need a suit; he was invulnerable, after all.

Their shared meals had become a quiet affair. They were run through. Between the training, the blog and planning for the fast-tracked mission, they all needed a break from conversation.

Liliana logged off the computer after sharing her latest article showing how egotistical Sentinel was and how that mindset didn't bode well to the city's future safety. All she wanted to do was grab a bite to eat and then collapse on her bed for a couple of hours before they needed to set off for the mission.

It would seem life had other plans. Her phone rang as she reached the kitchen. She wondered how the caller got through the base's protections.

"Ms Masters?" a familiar voice asked on the other end of the phone.

"This is she," Liliana replied.

"This is Detective Berkowitz." Liliana recognised the voice now.

"How can I help?" Liliana replied. Yates had just walked into the room and looked puzzled at Liliana. She put the phone on speakerphone for Yates to hear as well.

"I'm calling to let you know you need to come down to the station as soon as possible. We have a few more questions for you. Just routine, you understand." The detective sounded like she was trying to keep a calm, reassuring tone. But Liliana could tell she was stressed.

"Oh," Liliana replied. She didn't really have time for this. She still had to prepare for the mission.

"It will only take half an hour. So if you could make your way to the station at your earliest convenience, I would be very grateful."

"Okay. See you soon," Liliana replied, not sure when that would be. How could she fit this into everything else that needed doing?

"Thank you," Detective Berkowitz replied, hanging up the phone with a click. Liliana was left standing there, phone in hand, staring at Yates.

"What should I do?" Liliana asked.

"You should go. You need to maintain your cover; it could blow the mission if they suspect anything," Yates replied. Liliana could tell they were thinking a hundred miles a minute. Trying to figure out how this new appointment worked into their plans.

"Do we have the time for this?"

"It shouldn't be too long," Yates replied. "An hour to get there, have the interview and get back. You should still be able to get some rest before we head out tomorrow."

"Okay," Liliana replied. "Why do they want to see me now? I have done nothing to raise any suspicions."

"It's probably because they are moving Mr Victor the day after tomorrow. They want to assess you one more time to make sure you will not do anything," Yates rationalised.

"What's going on?" Johnathon asked as he entered the room with a plate stacked high with toast. Liliana's stomach grumbled at the sight.

"I have to go see the police. They want to question me again to make sure I'm not going to attempt a prison break."

"Which is exactly what you're planning to do," Johnathon replied.

"Precisely."

"So, you have to lie your ass off, to the police?" he asked.

"Yep."

"Good luck."

"Thanks, Johnathon. Really helpful," Liliana replied sarcastically. Resolved to having to tell a series of bald-faced lies to the authorities, Liliana grabbed her coat from the nearby coatrack and snatched a couple slices of toast from Johnathon's plate as she walked down to the garage.

"Hey!" Johnathon shouted after her.

"I'm hungry!" Liliana shouted back as she made her way down the stairs.

*

Driving through the city felt odd now. She was starting to understand what Max meant when he said he was watching over the city from Hilltop. She saw people going about their normal lives, unaware that she was the one sharing the truth of the Supers to everyone. She was showing them that the Supers were just like everyone else, fallible, and that they should be held to the same standards as everyone else.

It was an odd sense of power that she felt, almost like she was liberating everyone from the control of the Supers. She would have to monitor that feeling. It could get dangerous if left unchecked.

The city looked almost back to normal after the fight. The only remnants of the fight remained at the office building, the centre of the fight. She'd heard that there was a small memorial being kept nearby for the lives lost during the fight. She wondered if there was one for Johnathon.

She was half tempted to swing by the memorial on her way to the station, but she didn't have enough time. It was taking everything she had to stay calm about the mission. If all went well, she would see Max tomorrow. She could finally work through everything with him. Probably not what he would expect from their reunion, but it needed to happen.

She could only imagine his face as he saw she was

rescuing him. After his letter it would be the last thing he expected. That thought put a smirk on Liliana's face as she pulled into the station. Looking up at the building, she took a deep breath, keeping in mind the lies she was about to tell.

She walked up the steps to the station, running her lies through her mind, as a sudden gust of wind caught her purple coat. The gust ended as soon as it began. Liliana looked up at the sky, thinking a storm must be incoming for the wind to be that strong that suddenly. Not a cloud in sight. Strange.

She didn't even get to the receptionist before Detective Berkowitz walked out of her office to meet her.

"Ms Masters, thank you for coming down so quickly," she said, trying to seem friendly.

"No problem," Liliana replied, shaking the hand that was offered.

"If you'll just follow me." The detective led her down the corridor, same as last time. Liliana expected to be led to the same room, but they walked straight past that door. Instead, she was led to an interrogation room.

Liliana's heart rate increased as Detective Berkowitz held the door open for her. This was remarkably different from her last visit. They were both on edge, she could tell. What was going on? After a moment of hesitation, Liliana walked into the interrogation room, dreading what was going to come next. She just reminded herself that she had done nothing wrong. Yet.

"Why the change in location?" Liliana asked as she made her way to the far side of the table sat in the middle of the room. She turned as the detective closed the door behind her. Then she understood.

"I just wanted a little privacy for our chat," Sentinel replied. He had stood behind the door, making sure Liliana didn't see him until it was too late to turn back. So much for avoiding him at all costs. Now she was trapped in a room with him, with only Detective Berkowitz between them.

"Oh. I thought this was just an interview for the police?" Liliana asked Berkowitz.

"It is. But Sentinel has asked to take part as a member of the Super Taskforce. Given the subject of the interview, the Mayor has granted the Supers access to the case," Berkowitz replied, showing her unease at the situation. Liliana wondered if she might have found a friend in the detective after all.

"You've been difficult to track down, Ms Masters," Sentinel stated, sitting across from her at the table, hands folded in front of Liliana. He seemed relaxed, calm. It was unnerving.

"I didn't know you were trying to get ahold of me," she replied, testing him with a lie. Rose had warned her of course.

"Well, nevermind. We're here now, aren't we?" Sentinel replied.

"Yes. Here we are," Liliana replied, trying to seem relaxed as well, sure she was failing miserably. "How can I help?"

"I wanted to talk to you about our dear Max." Sentinel was being far too friendly for her liking. Detective Berkowitz sat to the side of the room, watching the two of them while remaining silent. She was simply a spectator to Liliana's interrogation.

"What about him?" Liliana asked, unsure of where Sentinel was going with this.

"Well, he's of the opinion that you've split with him. But I'm not so sure. I've heard how close the two of you were before this whole mess happened."

"How do you know what he thinks?" Liliana asked.

"I've had my fair share of conversations with him in the past couple of days," Sentinel replied.

So, he's been interrogating Max as well. Liliana hoped it had only been conversations. Without Max's suit Sentinel could have done some serious damage to him. Was he safe? Was there going to be anything of Max left for her to rescue?

"Max is right. We have split. He hid too much from me, you can't expect me to trust him after attacking the city like he did, can you?" Liliana lied. Well, it was partially a lie. She had mixed feelings after everything that had happened, but she was willing to talk it through with Max. To figure out where they now stood. If they could ever get back to the way things were.

"So, you're not planning anything? No fancy prison escape worthy of a blockbuster film?" Sentinel knew something was going on. But she wasn't about to confirm anything for him.

"Of course not, that would be stupid," Liliana replied, like she was pointing out the obvious.

"No lingering desire to see Max?" Sentinel pushed, waiting for her to slip up.

"Sentinel, I'm a journalist. I have no powers, no money to build special technology. I'm a good person, I wouldn't want to hurt anyone," she began. "So why on earth would I try to break a man out of prison, a man I have broken all ties with?"

Sentinel stared at her as she made her mini speech, taking in her words. Somehow, Liliana kept herself calm as she made her point. She stared him down, waiting for his response.

"Max has killed people. His actions almost killed me. I want nothing to do with him," Liliana forced herself to lie again. It was getting harder to say these things. She knew it was Sentinel who tried to kill her. It was likely him that killed the other people, not Max. These thoughts sank in as she stared at him. She was sat across from a killer. A man who tried to end her own life. How was she staying so calm? She was terrified and angry all at once. She stood no chance against Sentinel right now, and he knew it.

"I'll let him know you said that," Sentinel finally replied.

"Good." Her heart broke as she replied. She didn't want to hurt Max. She wanted to understand him. To help him. This was going to kill Max.

"As you're so set against Max, you should be happy to hear that there will be extra protection during his transfer. I won't be the only Super there. Just for peace of mind, you understand," Sentinel revealed.

"I wouldn't expect anything less," Liliana replied, happy to get some extra information on the move. They could be better prepared now.

"Thank you for coming down today. You've set my mind at rest knowing Max hasn't tainted your soul as well as his own," Sentinel ended the interrogation, his voice dripping with false honesty. Liliana was just happy to get away from him.

Chapter Twenty-Four

Rose focused on her computer, sorting through the latest batch of photographs she had taken. She was still working on the rebuild of the city, her latest photos showing the substantial progress that had been made. Sentinel helped a fair bit with the rebuild. He helped speed up the process and got some good press at the same time. Rose was sure that played a big part in his decision to help the builders.

She had also taken some snaps of the memorial which had been created around the corner from the temporary office they were still working in. The lives that were lost were the hardest part of the fight for her to rationalise. If Max wasn't the bad guy, why had people died? Sentinel was an ass, but would he let people die if he had the choice? She hoped not. Maybe neither of them was really the good guy. She did not know what to believe. Who to believe.

"Have you finished yet?" Tim asked, sitting down next to her. He was covering the same stories as her, and she hated it. At least he had finished hitting on her, she had got that point across, thankfully.

"Almost," she replied.

"I'll grab us some coffees while you finish up," Tim said, stretching as he stood up. Things had been uncomfortable but civil since his failed attempt at romance the other day. She was thankful that he wasn't pushing her for anything, romantic or otherwise. He seemed content now to let her get on and do her job.

She just hit upload on the last image, sending it to the paper's server, when Tim returned with the coffee.

"Here you go." Tim handed over her coffee and something about his hand caught her attention. A glint. Why would that attract her attention? There was nothing special about his hands. No scars, no blemishes. So, what was it?

She took the cup from him, thanking him as she did so, but her eyes remained on his hands while she tried to figure out what caught her attention. She took a sip as it hit her.

His nails. They shone slightly. Clear polish. She had seen these hands before. She choked on the sip of coffee as she realised what was going on.

"You okay there?" Tim asked, chuckling slightly as he patted her on the back, still choking on the coffee.

"I'm fine," she sputtered out, looking up at him, really looking at him. It all slid into place for her. She didn't know how she hadn't seen it before.

Tim was Sentinel.

The only things that were different were his clothes and that his hair was messy when he was Tim. But, somehow, that was all it took to look completely different.

"I need to go," Rose said, standing up quickly, dropping the coffee down on her desk as she made a quick retreat. Tim watched her go, a concerned look on his face.

What was she going to do with this information? What could she do? She couldn't carry on working with him like she didn't know. Her mind was racing a million miles a minute. This was too much to take in.

She needed to tell Liliana.

But how? She wasn't replying to her messages. They could meet up, but Sentinel had eyes on her for a while now. No. Tim had been watching her. Tim had been in her home last night. Sentinel asked her out. This was too much to handle. She needed a drink.

Tim versus Max. No wonder they clashed, they hated each other as themselves and as their alteregos. She wondered if Max knew who he was fighting. What was Tim going to do if he found out Rose knew? She'd already embarrassed him in front of all their co-workers. Someone egotistical enough to be Sentinel wasn't going to take that lying down.

She brought herself out of her thoughts to see that she had walked home without thinking about it. She hurried inside and locked the door behind her, foolishly thinking that might stop Tim if he came after her. She knew it wouldn't, but she refused to think about that possibility. She wouldn't stand a chance against him.

How was she going to go to work and face him now? Go about her normal life knowing who he really was? Knowing where he went when he would suddenly disappear under the guise of re-searching something for an article.

Come to it, how did he have the time to be a super-hero and the city's top reporter? Did he sleep? Did he eat? Well, he drank coffee, she knew that much. Was he even human? That question had never been officially answered about the Supers. Where did they get their powers from? They had always been extremely private about that information.

Rose opened the fridge and cracked open a fresh bottle of wine, sure she was going to drink most of it by the end of the day. She shouldn't be drinking in the middle of the day, but needs must.

What was she going to do?

*

Liliana pulled back into the garage, her heart heavy with regret for what she had said to Sentinel. She knew he was going to use her words to hurt Max, and she hated it. She had to focus on the fact that they were going to set him free, and she could tell him the truth then. Not long left to go.

She stared out of the windscreen at the concrete wall in front of her. Frozen while her mind and heart worked through the issues at hand. Or at least, they tried to work through. She felt trapped in an impossible situation, unable to move forward without risking everything.

She knew she had to get Max out, regardless of where they stood. He was innocent, mostly. Innocent enough to warrant the mission and o get him away from the danger Sentinel presented.

Why her? Why did this responsibility fall to Liliana? Because they ran into one another on that fateful day? The universe had bestowed a crappy path on her. Whatever decision they made going forward with their relationship, she was going to be on the dangerous side of the Supers. There was no way they would not figure out the prison break involved her.

She was still sitting in the car. She could easily drive away and forget everything. Her hands were on the wheel, the power button a quick movement away should she want to use it. She stared at the wall ahead of her, imagining what her life could be like if she left the mission here and now. She could drive away, start over in a new city, away from Sentinel. Forget Max and the situation he had put her in. She could take Rose with her, start over in a new paper together, the dream team.

The vision moved to imagine Max, stuck in prison for the rest of his life. Constantly in danger from Sentinel. She couldn't do that to him. If she left now, Yates and Johnathon would have to start over. It would be nigh on impossible to get to Max after his move. She would put them at risk if she didn't help. Her heart ached at the idea of leaving Max behind, alone, without knowing if they could have worked through this or not.

Even if they were to go their separate ways, she needed to know for sure. Resolved to see this entire mission through to the end, Liliana jumped out of the car before she could doubt again, slamming the door perhaps a little too hard in her determination.

Liliana took the steps faster than normal, racing up to see Yates and Johnathon in the living room, pouring over the plans once again. Johnathon was still catching up on all the work she and Yates had put into the plan. They had made some alterations when Johnathon revealed himself, but the plan worked better now that he was here. His powers made him a valuable friend to have.

"Ah, you're back. How did it go?" Yates asked,

stopping their conversation with Johnathon as she jogged into the room.

"Sentinel was there," Liliana cut to the chase.

"What? Why?" Johnathon asked, shocked at her revelation.

"He'd been trying to find me for a while now. He got bored and used the police to track me down," Liliana replied.

"Sneaky bastard," Johnathon replied.

"You can say that again," Liliana said.

Chapter Twenty-Five

Liliana could feel the clock working against her. The ambush from Sentinel had set her back, set them all back. There was still so much to do before the mission was ready. She hadn't finished her training, they needed to collect all the gear they would need, and they still needed some time to rest before it all kicked off. If Johnathon hadn't arrived when he did, they would have been well and truly screwed.

They had sent Liliana into the city to gather some supplies, food mainly. Yates was putting the final touches on their suits, and Johnathon was gathering all the tools they would need. He was enjoying exploring the base, just like Liliana did when she first got there. To be honest, there was probably more to be discovered, if only she had the time to explore properly.

She had run out to the closest supermarket to grab all the food they could need over the coming days, as well as some extras, just to be careful. Nothing perishable. Who knew what was going to happen after the prison break? They might not get back to the base straight away. If anyone looked in her basket right now, they would think she was preparing for the apocalypse or something.

The LED lights above Liliana shone down like a spotlight. Liliana felt like everyone was watching her prepare for a secret mission. Of course, there was no way anybody knew what she was planning. But that didn't stop her anxiety from rearing its ugly head against her. She could feel the pressure at the back of her throat, the small voice in the back of her head telling her that everyone knew. That they were going to stop her.

The air around her became thick as she fell into the thoughts she so desperately wanted to escape. She tried to focus on what she needed to do, but every time someone passed her in the shop, she became convinced they knew what was really going on. They were going to stop her.

No.

She tried to fight back against the monster that was her own mind. She reminded herself that there was no way they could know. Everyone believed the persona she had presented to the media. And they all believed whatever the media told them. The dad wrangling twin toddlers around the shop wasn't out to stop her. Neither was the pair of little old ladies buying milk. They were just ordinary people going about their ordinary lives.

The air began to cool and release the hold it had on

Liliana as she convinced herself that she was fine. She wasn't being watched, followed. Nobody was waiting for her to slip up. She focused back on her shopping list, quickly realising she should have got a trolley instead of a basket. Good thing she had been doing all those exercises. She was definitely stronger than she was before all this began. She pushed the last bit of pressure at the back of her throat back down as she looked around for the protein bars Yates had requested.

She turned down an empty aisle and ground to a halt as she noticed the man standing at the other end, walking towards her.

"Don't you have anyone to shop for you?" Liliana asked, shocked by the sarcasm showing in her voice.

"I actually prefer to do my own shopping. Normally more subtle than this, I have to admit," Sentinel replied with a smirk, coming to a stop a few paces in front of her. He looked in her basket, noting what she was buying. "Stocking up?"

"You think this is a lot? You should see what my brother went through growing up," Liliana lied through her teeth, trying to deflect from the obviously sizeable amount of food she was buying. She wasn't meant to be shopping for more than herself, as far as Sentinel was concerned.

"Max is being moved the day after tomorrow," Sentinel stated.

"I know," Liliana replied, unsure of where he was going with this.

"What do you have planned?" No hiding behind that question.

"For the day after tomorrow? More job hunting, I suppose," Liliana replied, not giving him anything.

"That all?" he asked.

"What else would there be?" she replied with her own question.

"Nothing, apparently," Sentinel replied, not breaking eye contact. He was trying to get her to slip up again. Didn't he learn from the first time? She wouldn't break.

They stood there for a minute or two, just staring at each other, each waiting for the other to break. Liliana could hear the hustle and bustle of the shop around them, but no one else was coming down their aisle. No one but her had noticed that the city's hero was in the local supermarket. The staring contest lasted longer than was truly necessary but soon, Sentinel broke.

"Good luck with the job hunt," he said before walking back down the aisle the way he came and disappearing around the corner.

Well, that was the weirdest encounter she'd had with Sentinel yet, she thought to herself. He was convinced she was planning something, but he had no proof. No idea she wasn't working alone.

He was expecting something clumsy, a pathetic attempt at a prison break. He wouldn't see them coming. Liliana allowed herself a small smirk at that thought as she went back to her shopping, wishing once more she had thought to get a trolley.

*

"Get everything we needed?" Yates asked as Liliana dumped her bags in the kitchen.

"I think so," she replied. "There was another ambush waiting for me."

"What?" Yates popped their head into the kitchen.

"Sentinel approached me in the middle of the supermarket," Liliana replied.

"That's rather brazen, don't you think?"

"Very. He is convinced I'm going to try something on my own," Liliana replied.

"You didn't break, I hope," Yates said.

"Of course I didn't," Liliana replied as she unloaded the shopping.

"Good. So, he doesn't know what's really going on then," Yates confirmed.

"No clue. He's expecting me to make a blundered attempt at a rescue. He probably won't be prepared for anything until we've already been in and out," Liliana said, smiling at the thought of Sentinel noticing them when it was already too late.

"Once you're done here, meet me in the gym," Yates ordered, walking out of the kitchen. Liliana shouted her reply while standing on the tips of her toes to store away the food. Someone definitely designed this kitchen with someone taller in mind, but Liliana was too stubborn to use the little footstall Yates had provided.

Once she finished, she refilled her water bottle and made her way down to the gym, fully expecting a last-minute training session. She wasn't disappointed as she saw Yates waiting for Liliana on the large mat in the middle of the room.

"Get changed." A simple order set Liliana's heart racing a little. She had been exercising and preparing for the mission, yet the idea of fighting Yates still made her nervous. She still had some bruises from their last training session, after all.

A moment later, Liliana was in her fighting gear, minus the suit, of course. Yates had arranged some slim fitting clothes, the perfect stretchy material for training and fighting. They covered her from neck to ankle, but they was breathable and cool. Yates stood on the mat across from Liliana, wearing a matching outfit, the only difference being the headscarf Yates wore.

Why was she more nervous about fighting Yates in a practice round than the mission tomorrow? She was in no real danger from Yates. But the way they stared down at her as they prepared for the sparring match was daunting, to say the least. Out of the corner of her eye, Liliana could see that Johnathon had joined them in the gym. He hesitated as he noticed they were about to fight, but then found a seat along the back wall and settled in to watch.

Great, now I have an audience, Liliana thought to herself, wishing Johnathon hadn't joined them. She didn't have long to get annoyed with Johnathon before Yates launched into an attack. Liliana dodged the attack, sliding around to the side, letting Yates carry on past where she had been standing. As Liliana moved to the side, she twisted and threw her leg out to make contact. But Yates had moved out of reach too quickly.

Liliana took a couple steps backwards to reassess quickly, then she launched into an attack of her own. Previously, she had been mainly defensive, but she wanted to try something different today, to work through the stress she was feeling. Yates had a brief look of surprise at her change in tactics but blocked her attacks easily.

Liliana was consistently trying to land hits on Yates, punch after jab, but nothing was landing. Yates was blocking her while getting in a few jabs of their own. Liliana's ribs were feeling the fight, she needed to make a move soon, otherwise Yates would have her on the mat again. She needed this win. An idea popped into her head, and it only took a split-second decision to follow through. Liliana threw a left-handed punch, knowing it wouldn't land. As the punch was blocked, she dropped to one knee and hooked her right arm under Yates's right leg and yanked, hard. That knocked Yates off their feet, taking their own hard fall onto the mat.

Before Yates had a moment to get their feet back underneath them Liliana rolled them onto their front and pinned their arms behind their back. Climbing on top of them, Liliana used her feet to trap Yates's legs, using everything she had to stop Yates from wriggling free of her hold.

"Nice move!" Johnathon shouted from the sidelines.

Yates nodded in agreement, motioning for Liliana to let them up again. Liliana stood and offered Yates a hand up. Pleased she could finally defeat Yates, she wasn't ashamed to say she was a bit too proud of herself for the victory.

"Yes, well done, Ms Masters," Yates said, catching their breath. "You've improved nicely. Good tactics in the heat of battle."

"Thanks. I still couldn't land a punch, though," Liliana replied.

"Fighting isn't all about hitting. There are many methods to success," Yates said. "You are good with problem solving, add that to the tech in your suit and you're well prepared for tomorrow." Liliana couldn't help but puff out her chest a little in pride. It meant a lot to hear that from Yates; it helped to ease her stress about the mission. She might actually stand a chance of coming through this crazy plan.

Chapter Twenty-Six

Liliana met Yates and Johnathon in the living room after a scoldingly hot shower, which was very much needed after her sparring match with Yates. They all needed to go over the plans one last time before the big day tomorrow. Liliana was both excited and stressed out by the impending deadline.

"Sentinel is expecting an escape plan to happen the day of the move, which is why we will move in just before dawn tomorrow, a full twenty-four hours before he's ready," Liliana began the discussion. She checked the clock on the wall and noted the time. "We have twelve hours until the mission begins. We need to make sure everything is packed and ready and get some rest ourselves."

"We'll all go in together, through the singular breach point," Yates said, pointing at the underground car park they had spotted on their reconnaissance missions. "Then, we'll split off into our designated positions. Once we have Mr Victor, we will make a hasty retreat. No fighting unless it's absolutely necessary."

"That's right, we don't want any bloodshed. Max already has a poor reputation with everything that's happened, we don't want to make it worse," Liliana agreed. If they could show that Max was harmless, even during a prison break, it would help his image.

"Johnathon, your suit is ready for you." Yates turned to Johnathon. "I admit, it doesn't do too much, it doesn't need to. But it will protect your identity."

"Thank you." Johnathon was grateful for the effort Yates had gone to for him. "I have little in the way of family, but I want to protect what I do have." He looked relieved yet prepared for the mission. Liliana was glad Johnathon had joined them but even happier to know that Johnathon had found a purpose. He had admitted to her he didn't know what to do with himself, with his powers. This mission had given him a path forward.

"If all goes well, we should be back here tomorrow morning with Max," Liliana concluded. Then the fun would begin.

*

Rose knew something was going to happen. She felt it in her gut. Liliana was planning something and it was about to go down. She wasn't going to wait until moving day to make a move. She wasn't that stupid. The stress was getting to be too much, waiting to hear what she had done, if they had captured her. Rose loved Max; she knew he was a good guy down to his soul. But this was too much. Liliana was going to go too far, she just knew it.

Rose sat in her living room, watching the news, just waiting for the story to break. An attempted prison break, perpetrators captured, soon to be named. She picked up her phone and opened her contacts to Liliana's number, sorely tempted to call her to put a stop to whatever she was planning.

But as soon as she would make that call, she would put a massive target on both their backs. Liliana was only suspected right now. If Rose tried to stop her, her guilt would be confirmed. And they would take Rose down with her.

She had to leave Liliana to her choices if she were to have any chances of success. Rose hated it, she felt next to useless. She sat hunched forward over her phone, stuck in her indecision, heart and mind telling her different things. Oblivious to her surroundings as she fought with her conflicting emotions.

She didn't hear the window crack open behind her, or the soft steps on her thick carpet. She didn't notice the figure looming over her as she stared at her phone, willing Liliana to make the right decision without her input.

Just as she started to gain awareness of her surroundings and think something wasn't quite right, the world went dark, and she slid into unconsciousness. The figure lifted her limp body and snuck back out of the apartment, Rose's neighbours none the wiser.

*

"Is everything packed?" Yates asked, standing in the middle of several packs spread around the living room, checklist in hand.

"It would appear so," Liliana replied as she dropped the last bag. "Do we actually need all of this stuff?"

Considering they were aiming for a stealthy in-and-out job, they were taking a lot with them. Thankfully, there was a spacious van tucked away in the garage below them to use.

"Some of it is for the mission, some of it is in case we get separated from the base after the mission. Overly cautious, I know, but better safe than sorry," Yates explained.

"So, we're packing for the worst-case scenario?" Johnathon asked.

"No, worst-case scenario is we're all captured and locked up alongside Max," Liliana answered.

"I'm trying my hardest not to picture that," Johnathon replied, his face going a little pale at the thought of being behind bars. It would be bad enough for Liliana and Yates, but Johnathon's powers would set him apart in prison. They would keep him beyond supermax. The Supers themselves would see to his incarceration. That wouldn't be fun at all.

"Let's load the van up, try to keep our minds off that thought, shall we?" Yates said, bringing Liliana and Johnathon out of their dark thoughts for a little while longer.

They all grabbed as many bags as they could carry and loaded up the van, what might be their home for a while after they completed the mission. Of course, they hoped they would get back here with no issue. But when you have the Supers involved, things could easily get messy.

Once they finished, they all collapsed on the sofa back in the living room. The van had been spacious when they started, but if there were going to be four of them bunched in, it was going to be a tight squeeze.

"It feels like we're forgetting something," Liliana said, staring up at the high ceiling from her position on the sofa.

"I always feel like that before a mission," Yates replied. They often made comments like that, almost enticing Liliana to ask about their past.

"Have you been on many missions?" Johnathon asked, having the courage Liliana clearly didn't have.

"A few," Yates replied, raising their eyebrows at Johnathon's prying question. "I had a fairly unconventional upbringing compared to you two."

Liliana sat up, wondering if she was finally going to hear some details of Yates's mysterious past. She wasn't even sure if Max was brave enough to ask questions.

"What sort of missions?" Johnathon was stupid or brave, or both. Liliana couldn't decide.

"Oh, this and that. Deliveries, collections, anything really," Yates replied. Their eyes glinted mischievously, hinting at the level of detail they were leaving out to their answers.

"Are you going to give us any details?" Johnathon pried once more.

"Maybe one day," Yates answered before hesitating a little. "But I will say this." They leant forward, drawing Johnathon and Liliana's attention in. Liliana sat up and gave Yates her full attention.

"This isn't the first time I've been on a mission to save Mr Victor. In fact, it's how we first met."

"Oh! You can't leave it at that!" Liliana exclaimed, jaw dropping at what they could mean.

"Mr Victor got himself in a spot of trouble. They sent me to sort it out," Yates replied, not giving any details away. "Although, my employer at the time wasn't too pleased with how I sorted it out. He wanted a more permanent solution."

"He wanted Max dead?" Liliana asked, enthralled by Yates's tale. "What did Max do?"

"He may have flirted with the wrong person's

wife," Yates replied, smirking a little. "But that's all I'll say on the matter."

She couldn't believe it. Max flirted with a woman and almost got himself killed. She loved him, but he was an idiot sometimes.

"What made you decide to let him live?" She couldn't help but ask more questions. Yates just smiled as they reminisced about their first meeting with Max.

"We had a friendly conversation. He made some good points and offered me a job," Yates replied. "He can be a smooth talker when he really wants to be."

"That he can," Liliana laughed. She finally felt relaxed, just what she needed before the mission tomorrow. She glanced over at the clock high on the wall. "It's getting late, we need to get some sleep before tomorrow."

She stood and said goodnight to Johnathon and Yates. She could tell Johnathon wanted to ask more questions. He had the true soul of a reporter, always wanting more details. Liliana, on the other hand, had learnt when the right time for questions was, and when to let go.

As she climbed into bed, she thought of the letter Max had written to her before they caught him. She pulled it out of the bedside table, kept safe. She read the words again, for the hundredth time since she had received the letter.

Pouring over Max's words, she couldn't help but wish he were already there with her. He felt so close, yet so far away. She pictured Max locked up a couple of miles away from her. Perhaps he was lying in bed as well, thinking about her. She wished she could tell him she still loved him, that she believed him. Instead, he believed that she had thrown him aside after the fight. Her chest hurt with the thought that she had broken his heart. Not long left now, she thought, wishing Max to hear her as well.

Chapter Twenty-Seven

"Oh Maxie, this is no time to sleep," Sentinel called through the bars of the prison cell.

"What do you want?" Max grumbled, sitting up from his tiny bed. "It's the middle of the night."

"I just wanted to check in and see how you were doing," Sentinel replied, false positivity running through his words.

"Same as always. Locked up for doing the right thing," Max replied with the same tone, just trying to annoy Sentinel.

They stood opposite each other, only the bars separating them. But they both knew that wouldn't stop Sentinel if he really wanted to get in. Max stood there in the typical bright-orange prison jumpsuit; Sentinel stood proudly in his costume.

"I think we can debate that, can't we?" Sentinel replied, trying to seem taller than Max against the bars. "I would say your beloved public would say you're right where you belong."

"That's because you've brainwashed them, Sentinel," Max replied. "We've been through this time and time again. You know the truth; you just won't let them see it."

"Are you still clinging to that? You're alone in your thinking," Sentinel said. He was trying to taunt Max into an argument again.

"The truth? I will always cling to the truth, as long as I have breath I will shout it to anyone that will listen," Max replied, knowing full well what Sentinel was trying to do. But this was his only way to fight back now. He had no way of escaping. No one was coming for him. Even Yates was powerless to help him in here.

"No one's listening to you anymore. Not even your precious Liliana," Sentinel said, aiming where it truly hurt.

Max had been heartbroken to hear that Liliana was moving on without him. He wouldn't have believed Sentinel if he hadn't seen the reports himself. The footage of her out enjoying herself with Rose. While he knew they would not date each other, he knew she had moved on; she didn't believe him. He hated he had lost her, but if she was happy and safe, then he could live with what he had done. It killed him to know he would never see her again. But he just wanted Liliana to be safe. If Sentinel believed their fight to be over, then maybe he wouldn't go after her again.

If only Max hadn't slipped up the other week, then maybe Sentinel wouldn't have figured out who he was. Sentinel was watching the Mayor's speech. He had heard what Max had said. Then, when they fought later that day, Max had slipped and repeated himself, allowing Sentinel to put two and two together. If Max had worked out who Sentinel really was, then maybe he could have beaten Sentinel at his own game.

Maybe someday he would be exposed for what he truly was, a power-hungry dictator. Max hoped someone else would carry on with his work, whoever they may be. He needed to be stopped before he controlled the entire city. Once he had the city, it wouldn't be long before he moved his sights to a higher seat of power. Of course, he had been recruiting for his new Taskforce. Max still believed that the Supers needed to be stopped.

"If only Liliana had her own powers. Then I'm sure I could find a place for her on my team," Sentinel carried on, trying to rile Max up.

"Just because she doesn't believe in me anymore doesn't mean she would believe in you," Max replied.

"Are you so sure about that?" Sentinel jabbed. "Your betrayal might have swayed her to my side. You don't know what's been happening the last couple of days. We've had some pleasant chats."

"You've spoken to Liliana?" Max grabbed the bars and pulled himself closer to Sentinel.

"Yes, well, I had to be sure she wasn't harbouring

a secret plan to get you out when we move you to-morrow, of course," Sentinel replied, happy to have Max listening intently.

"Is she ok?"

"She's adamantly against you, you know," Sentinel said with a smug smile. "Enough, maybe, for us to grow a little closer, perhaps."

"Don't you go anywhere near her," Max growled through the bars. The idea of the two of them to-gether was abhorrent.

"It can't be helped if she falls into my open arms, heartbroken by your actions," Sentinel teased. He was enjoying their conversation far too much. "She's had a villain, why not a hero?"

Max thrust his arms through the bars, trying to reach Sentinel, who stepped back just enough to be out of reach. He laughed at Max's attempt to stop him. He got what he wanted, a worked-up Max, angry at his words.

"Keep your lying hands off of her!" Max yelled, frustrated that he couldn't reach Sentinel. He was powerless behind the bars.

Sentinel just chuckled at the agony he had caused before walking off, leaving Max to shout after him, unable to do anything about his situation. After Sentinel had left Max's sight and he was once again all alone, he couldn't help but break.

Max collapsed to his knees, tears streaming down

his face. He wished he still had Liliana by his side. He should have been honest with her from the start, then he wouldn't have lost her. He crumbled as he realised he would never see her brilliant smile again, never feel her healing hugs, never be able to enjoy her company.

*

Coffee was everywhere once all three of them were awake. Waking up while the city below them still slumbered, dreaming random thoughts, required a lot of caffeine. Despite the sheer amount they had prepared and packed the afternoon before, there was still a mad rush to get ready to head out.

The clock had run out. This was their time to act. No more sparring matches, no more plans to make. Now they had to enact the plans they had spent hours pouring over. The anticipation was palpable in the base. Everyone was a messy mix of excitement and nerves. Even Yates, in all their worldliness, seemed on edge with it all.

Liliana pulled her hair tight into a hair tie. The last thing she needed for the mission was to be blinded by her own long, dark hair. She was sure it was frizzy as hell, being pulled back like that with no product, but she wasn't aiming for a good look. Purely practical on mission day. She almost envied Johnathon with his short back and sides, and Yates's headscarf. Both very helpful on such an important mission.

Liliana was lost in her own world as she prepared to ship out for the prison. She almost missed the noise her phone made, lying on the coffee table where she left it the night before. They weren't bringing phones with them as it could track her outside of the base. A message had popped through on her lock screen. Liliana wondered who it could be. Rose hadn't messaged her in a while, as she was being watched too closely. Liliana picked up the phone out of sheer curiosity.

It was her mother.

Why on earth was her mother texting her? They hadn't spoken since their argument in the hospital room the other week.

Mother: *Liliana, I am writing to let you know your cousin Maria has an opening in her shop. If you are still looking for a job, she would be happy to give you an interview.*

Well, that was the weirdest message she could have got right before carrying through with a prison break plan. Liliana paused in her astonishment. Her mother, formal as always over text, completely ignoring the last words shared between them. Suggesting that she interview for a shop assistant job with her cousin. A bit of a change from her career as a journalist.

She didn't even know how to respond to that message; she stood there staring at the message.

"Everyone alright?" Johnathon asked as he joined

her in the living room, ready for the mission.

"Just a message from my mother."

"Oh?" Johnathon didn't know about her relationship with her mother, so this must seem like a normal situation to him.

"Telling me that my cousin wants to interview me for her shop," Liliana said, half chuckling at the absurdity of the message.

"What's so funny about that?" Johnathon furrowed his brow in confusion.

"Well, the last time we spoke I came out as bisexual to my incredibly religious and conservative mother. Or rather, I shouted it at her from a hospital bed. We haven't spoken since," Liliana explained.

"Ah. That must have been awkward." He looked concerned. "I take it she didn't react well, then?"

"Not really. She just stormed out of the room," Liliana continued. "I wasn't surprised, given how she always treated Rose."

"Oh, is Rose bi as well?" Johnathon asked.

"Gay, actually. We dated for a while," Liliana replied. Normally she wouldn't discuss the sexual orientation of others, but Rose was out and proud. She wouldn't mind Liliana confirming the truth. "You didn't really get to know her before this all happened, did you?"

"No. She seems like a lovely person, though a little scary," Johnathon said.

"Hey!" Yates shouted as they saw Liliana and Johnathon chatting. "We don't have time for sitting around. Get moving!"

Liliana and Johnathon almost jumped out of their skins as Yates shouted at them. They were right, though; they needed to get moving. Dawn was a couple of hours away, and they needed to get in and out before the sun caught up with them.

Chapter Twenty-Eight

The ride to the prison was tense. With every turn they made, Liliana expected to come across a blockade of some kind. Or see Sentinel standing in the street ahead of them, ready to stop them. But the roads were blissfully quiet. Everyone was still sleeping as they wound their way through the city towards the prison on the outskirts.

There was no direct path to the prison from the base unless you wanted to go seriously cross country. But that would be fairly obvious in their van. At the moment, they just looked like a worker getting an early start to the day.

Liliana looked at the quiet city as they drove through the familiar streets. She felt like she was viewing the city from a different perspective today. Technically, she was about to become a criminal, or vigilante. It depended on your stance on the Supers. If it became known that she was involved in the prison break, she wouldn't be able to just walk around the city freely again. She would hide with Max, at least until they could clear his name.

They had planned nothing for after the prison

break just yet. It seemed silly to, with such an important step to take first. She hoped they would end up in a position to do some good in the city, to help clear Max's name and reputation. And to help Liliana's reputation at the same time. How they were going to expose the Supers for what they were, she did not know.

So many possibilities faced her but with one big question mark blocking her path. The prison break. She needed to focus on the mission before she could get obsessed with their next steps. She berated herself for getting distracted by the city lights instead of focusing on the mission.

Yates was behind the wheel, steering them through the city, with Johnathon sitting in the back with all the bags. It couldn't have been very comfortable, but he was stubbornly gentlemen about the decision to sit in the back. Liliana didn't feel too bad about taking the comfy seat up front. She could get bruises from the bags, Johnathon wouldn't.

They turned down the last main street in the city before it released them to the outskirts. Liliana could almost see the bright lights used to see the outer rim of the prison in the distance.

"Not far now," Yates commented.

"Good to know," Johnathon replied loudly in the back. The van turning around the corner led to another loud thud. "I'm getting beaten up by the equipment back here."

"You can take it, Mr Invulnerable," Liliana shouted back, laughing a little at Johnathon's expense, trying to lighten the mood.

"Okay, if I end up with a superhero name, please don't let that be it," Johnathon replied, a begging tone carrying through his voice.

"Oh, no? What sort of name would you like then?" Liliana asked.

"I don't know. Something that hints at my power without saying it outright?" Johnathon shouted back. "Something like Dragonhide."

"Dragonhide?" Liliana replied. "That's a ridiculous name. You aren't a dragon, nor do you look like one."

"Maybe not, but it's cool, don't you think?" Johnathon tried to convince her. All it did was remind Liliana how much younger Johnathon was to her and Yates.

Liliana looked over at Yates to see them trying their hardest not to laugh at Johnathon.

"Why have you gone quiet?" Johnathon asked, a little panicked. "Wait! Are you two laughing at me?"

"No," Liliana replied as the laughing broke free from the both of them. Laughing right before this kind of mission didn't feel right, but it felt good.

"You guys are so mean to me sometimes," Johnathon shouted over the laughter.

"Sorry," Liliana tried to keep the laughter under control. "But that wasn't the best name, to be honest. We don't live in a fantasy world after all."

"Yeah, yeah. Whatever," Johnathon replied, slightly annoyed that they had shot his suggestion down hard.

"You'll come up with something better than that, I'm sure of it," Yates called back, finally getting their laughter under control.

They were finally getting close to the prison; it was tucked away at the bottom of the hill they were driving down.

"Liliana, I think it's time for you to climb in the back with Johnathon," Yates said. Liliana unbuckled herself, something she wouldn't have done a couple of weeks ago. A daredevil. She climbed into the back with Johnathon, almost falling on him in the process.

"Not as easy as they make it look in the movies," Liliana commented as Johnathon helped steady her against the van wall.

"Pull that screen across and start the hacking programme on the computer," Yates ordered as they started down the long drive to the security gate.

They had fit the van with a whole host of stealth tech which Max's company had been working on for several years now. Liliana pulled the canvas screen across the width of the van, cutting them off from Yates. It blinked to life to let her and Johnathon see through partially. Yates had previously told them that anyone on the other side would only see a van full to the brim with boxes. Boxes they were supposedly delivering to the prison. It was an amazing piece of technology. Liliana was surprised the military hadn't claimed it yet.

Johnathon had opened and booted up the computer they had packed the previous night. Yates had organised the software to be user friendly. All Johnathon had to do was set it running once they pulled up to the gate. It should update their system to let them all in. Liliana could feel Yates slowing down to pull up to the checkpoint.

"ID," a voice shouted through the little booth.

"Here you go." Yates handed over what was hopefully a convincing fake ID card. Johnathon tapped on his keyboard a couple of times as the guard checked Yates's ID. He was so focused on the screen. Liliana almost asked him if it was working a couple of times. She had to stay quiet. She didn't want the guard to hear her over the van's engine.

The guard was taking his time checking the ID; he was sending Liliana's nerves through the roof. She began nervously tapping her hand against her leg, quietly, but radiating anxiety at the same time. She didn't stop until Johnathon let out a breath of relief. He looked up from the computer and nodded at Liliana. They were in.

The van shuddered to life once more as they were allowed through the first set of gates. They had to pause for a moment to be shut between the two sets of gates before being let through to the underground car park. Step one was complete. Step two involved an ingenious piece of software left behind in the guard's station computer. A piece of software that would come in very handy when it came to them escaping together.

While Yates found them a parking spot, Johnathon and Liliana grabbed the bag they would need for the next stage, yet more tech that Liliana didn't really understand. They had suited up before heading out earlier that morning, something Liliana was thankful for. The idea of suiting up in the cramped van didn't really need entertaining.

A bang reverberated around them in the van. Yates pulled the side door open, letting them out into the car park. They had timed their arrival correctly; the car park was virtually empty this time in the morning.

"Johnathon, head up to the security office. Stay on comms at all times," Yates said, handing Johnathon the bag after taking some gauntlets out and strapping them to their wrists. "Liliana, you follow me through security and we'll find Mr Victor."

Together they activated their suit helmets, hiding

their faces from the guards in the prison above them. Liliana looked at the three of them, stood next to the van filled with their back up supplies, knowing there was no going back now. Not that she would want to.

Johnathon headed upstairs before them, pulling out a small handheld device from the bag and activating it as soon as the door from the stairwell was open. The guards in the nearby security office passed out as the device let out a wave designed to render anyone nearby unconscious. Yates had built in shields to their suits, useful in case anyone else had similar technology.

Johnathon moved into the security room, dragging the three guards to the side of the room and tying them up. He didn't want anyone waking up before they were meant to, that could get messy. He had control of the prison complex's security system. That felt far too easy to him.

"You're all clear," Johnathon said through the comms system in his suit.

"Quick, nicely done," Liliana replied.

She and Yates made their way up through the staircase, moving past the security room where Johnathon waved them through.

"Any sign of Supers?" Yates asked.

"Nothing yet," Johnathon replied, checking over the cameras.

"Keep us in the loop."

"According to their system, Max is in Cell Block D. He's the only one in there."

"Is that weird?" Liliana asked. Why would Max have his own cell block? Surely, if nothing else, he would have been placed with the other people Sentinel and the Supers had captured over the years.

"It's a little odd, I'll admit," Yates replied as they crept through the corridor after Johnathon. "Keep your eyes peeled for a surprise attack."

A surprise attack, just what they wanted. A small part of Liliana had hoped they would get in and out without a fight, just using the tech Max had designed to bypass the obstacles a prison presented.

The prison was quiet around them. The small number of guards on the night shift were all sleeping in the room behind them, the prisoners were out in their cells. Yates and Liliana made their way down the corridor quietly, footsteps muffled by their suits.

After they passed a long row of cells, they reached a crossroad.

"Max is to your right." Johnathon was guiding them through the labyrinth that was the prison. Before they could take the right-hand option, they heard a noise coming from their left. Someone was on the move down to the left.

"Johnathon, anything on the cameras?" Yates

asked.

"Nothing's coming up. There's something odd about this feed. It keeps blinking at me."

Yates and Liliana realised the problem at the same time.

"It's a recording," they said together.

"Someone could be down there, coming for us," Liliana whispered, as if they could hear her talk. What were they going to do now?

"I'll check it out," Yates decided. "You carry on and find Mr Victor, continue with the mission as planned. Rendezvous back at the van once it's all done."

"Okay," Liliana agreed, hating the fact she was now on her own. She reluctantly turned her back on Yates as they explored the side of the prison they hadn't planned for. She faced the next corridor, which seemed even more daunting now she was alone.

Chapter Twenty-Nine

Yates stalked down the dim corridor, Liliana walked away behind them. Someone was down here and it wasn't just the prisoners that were being suspiciously quiet. All the guards had been accounted for, so who was it? Had Sentinel posted some of the Taskforce here o watch over Mr Victor?

"I know you're here somewhere," a voice called through the darkness. Yates had always been quiet on their feet, able to sneak about without being noticed, but their nerves seemed to be affecting that talent tonight. Yates remained silent, trying to get a better sense of the voice before making any decisions.

A light shone through the small windows above them, moving across the corridor towards Yates. The searchlight was swinging around, trying to find a hint of a break-in.

"Where are you hiding?" the voice called through the darkness, quiet yet easily carried down the corridor.

The searchlight shone on a figure slowly stepping down the corridor, red boots making barely a sound with each step. The light cast a strong figure. Armour? Yates couldn't tell.

Yates crouched down near an empty cell, trying to assess the figure calling out to them. They could see a hint of a cape draped behind the red boots. They were a Super. Or someone who fancied themselves a Super. Which one, Yates couldn't tell.

"Going by your silence, I'm going to guess you're Max's reserved bodyguard," the figure continued to talk to the darkness. "What's your name again? Bates?" The figure kept creeping closer and closer to their hiding spot. Soon enough they would be spotted. Especially if the searchlight kept swinging around. Yates needed to make a move, and soon.

"It's Yates, actually," they replied, stepping back, keeping to the shadows. Waiting for the figure to make their first move, to show who they are.

A light flickered to life just ahead of Yates, hovering around the figure's left hand. Fire.

"And you're Lightbringer. Good to know," Yates stated, grabbing for the devices Mr Victor had designed for this particular Super. Two blocks resembling gun clips attached to their wrists, ready to be aimed and fired at Lightbringer.

"I would have thought a powerless human like you would be running right now." Lightbringer stepped fully into the swinging searchlight, confirming who she was. "But I guess you aren't as smart as Max made you out to be."

She stood, confident of her victory already, a red cape fluttering behind her bright-white suit. Her arms were exposed to keep clear of the fire she could command at will. Her platinum blonde hair was braided back, a streak of red winding through one side of her head. The red continued down to colour her eyes and her lips, pulled up into a smirk.

"I'm just wondering how on earth people believe you're the good guy when you look like that," Yates shot back, admitting to themselves that the devilish appearance was a bit much for a so-called superhero.

"Oh, sweetie, I'm gorgeous," Lightbringer replied, her voice dripping in threats.

"Don't call me sweetie," Yates replied as Lightbringer prepared to attack.

Lightbringer threw her arms up in unison, bright flames quickly forming at the ends of her closed fists, aimed directly at Yates. In return, Yates lifted their own arms, aiming the specially designed weapons back at her.

They shot flames and countermeasures simultaneously, meeting together in the hallway, which was lit up by the fire. Yates wasn't sure how much fire suppressants they had at their disposal, hopefully it would be enough to put Lightbringer down.

Hot met cold in the middle of the corridor, each

one vying for triumph. Lightbringer threw everything she had into her fire stream, trying to power through the fire suppressants. However, Mr Victor had designed this weapon to release at a higher velocity to Lightbringer's fire. Soon enough, the fire died down to just cover Lightbringer's fingers. It flickered, struggling to survive under Yates's counterattack.

Struggling for breath, Lightbringer stumbled back slightly. She hadn't planned for a counterattack, especially not one designed for her specific powers. Yates took the opportunity while they had it and leapt forward, landing a punch on the side of her face, knocking her to the floor.

This was new to Lightbringer, no one had ever got close enough to make contact before. Her eyes swam in and out of focus as she tried to fight back.

"Stay down," Yates ordered. Lightbringer slowly nodded her head. She wasn't going to be fighting-fit anytime soon. Yates stepped back, making sure that Lightbringer wouldn't follow them. They jogged back along the corridor, trying to catch up with Liliana.

*

Moonlight shone through the top windows in a stark contrast to the thick concrete walls they were positioned in. The cells she walked past were dark, too dark for her to see if they were occupied or not. The corridor was never ending, cell upon cell upon cell, locked away where no one could see them.

She found it hard to remind herself that most people locked away in a prison were actually guilty of various crimes. The system should work, but it didn't right now. Yet another thing that would need to change.

Focus. She needed to focus. She needed to find Max, they were so close to finishing this mission. One corner left and she should be in the right place to find Max.

"The doors are all open for you, Liliana," Johnathon said, almost making her jump.

"Any word from Yates yet?" she asked.

"Nothing yet. They aren't showing up on the cameras either. Something is definitely up with my feed," Johnathon replied. "I can't see anything ahead of you, but we can't really trust that right now. Be careful."

"You too," she replied, unsure of what else to say.

Liliana walked through one set of open doors, around the corner to the left, and through another set of doors. She expected a lot of security, but even this seemed overkill to her. The way ahead was empty, no Supers, no guards. Nothing standing between her and Max but a cell door.

That was the wrong thing to think. A figure stepped out ahead of her, blocking her path to

Max. There wasn't much light in the corridor, but enough to show her who she was up against.

"I knew you were going to do something like this," Sentinel said, rolling his shoulders, clearly ready for a fight.

"Then why did you bother coming?" Liliana tried to inject a bit of ego into her taunt, not that she really expected it to work against Sentinel. His ego was big enough for the both of them. In response, Sentinel smirked and shifted his position into a fighting stance. This was what Liliana had wanted to avoid at any cost, but he stood in her way.

Liliana's viewscreen switched to fight mode and she launched into an attack. While the suit did not add to her speed to match Sentinel, it boosted the strength of her attack. She used the boosters to throw the first punch, aimed at the centre of Sentinel's stomach, intended to wind him.

She made Sentinel take a step back. Better than she expected, but not as much of a reaction as she hoped.

"You're packing quite the punch there. Max's tech?" Sentinel asked, turning to grab her as she darted past. She barely slipped through his fingers.

"Perhaps," she replied, ducking under Sentinel's swinging arm, a fumbled attempt to knock her down. Sentinel next moved to grab her with both arms, putting a bit of speed behind the move. Liliana dropped to a knee, letting him fly over her.

She helped by using the boosters in her legs to force Sentinel to go flying over her and tumbling to the floor.

Not wanting to give Sentinel a moment to recover his position, Liliana immediately turned and threw another punch. This one aimed at his head as he lay spread across the floor. He was too quick this time, her fist hit the floor where his head once was.

He stepped back to put some space between the two of them, wiping a drop of blood from the corner of his mouth. Not used to bleeding for a human, he had a calculating look on his face, staring at the suit Liliana was wearing as if he were trying to find a way to defeat it. He clearly didn't expect the fight to last more than a single hit on his part. While Liliana had yet to land a single punch, she was feeling exhilarated by the fight. The adrenaline was rushing through her body, egging her on in the fight.

Now was the time, she decided, to see what toys she had to play with in the suit. The viewscreen, intuitive as always, brought up a list of options. The light bomb. Nope, that was for Glassier. Fire suppression system. Nope, that was for Lightbringer. Where were the Sentinel specific options?

Aha! There was a good option. Sentinel couldn't see any better than a regular human in the dark. Liliana activated the smoke screen, a remarkable piece of tech designed to cover the immediate area in thick, black smoke too dense to see even your hand right in front of you. Liliana had the advantage now, her suit allowed her to see through the smoke where no one else could.

"Ah, nice choice!" Johnathon said through the comms. He was watching their fight through the security cameras. Liliana wanted to ask about Yates, but she couldn't shift her attention away from the fight right now.

"Smart move. But it won't work," Sentinel called through the smoke, looking around, trying to find her. He was blind. He was trying to get her to respond and give away her position. But Yates had trained her better than that. Liliana moved as quietly as she could to get as close to Sentinel as she could before trying to knock him out.

She flicked through her next possible moves. She could try hitting him again but that didn't have much of an effect the last time. She didn't think tying him up would work. He was too strong to stay in cuffs, even the special ones Yates had built into the suit. A moment later, she had the perfect option, she smiled to herself as she decided. He wouldn't see this coming. Liliana snuck behind Sentinel, leaving him to wave his arms around, trying to find her.

"Where have you gone?" Sentinel called through the smoke, unaware that she was right behind him. She raised her arm, prepping the needle for her next move. Aimed for the back of his neck, which was foolishly exposed, she fired. "What the?" Sentinel grabbed for the back of his neck, pulling out the small dart, but not before it let loose the most powerful sedative Yates had found. They had hoped it would be enough to take Sentinel down, if needed, but they did not know how long it would last. Sentinel sank to his knees, looking at the dart in his hands.

"Impossible," he said as he fell flat on his face, out cold. Just in time as well; the smoke screen was fading quickly. Liliana couldn't help but let out a sharp laugh, celebrating her success. She didn't have long, though, she needed to get Max and get out before the drug made its way through Sentinel's system.

"Which one is he in?" Liliana asked Johnathon. A door three ahead of where she stood clicked in response. Her heart skipped a beat. This was it. She walked in front of the open door as she saw a figure move inside.

"What the?" Max said, clambering to his feet in surprise.

"Long time no see," Liliana said, adding that extra little bit of shock to Max's reaction. She opened her helmet to show Max who she was.

"What on earth are you doing here?" Max said, rushing forward to embrace Liliana.

"Rescuing you, of course," Liliana replied simply. All she wanted was to sink into the hug, to wrap her arms around Max and never let go. But she was very much aware of where they were stood. They still had to escape together.

"I thought— The news— I didn't think you accepted my letter," Max stumbled through his words, not believing that she stood right in front of him.

"I'm an excellent actress, aren't I?" Liliana replied. "We need to get moving. Sentinel is in the corridor, unconscious for now."

"What!" Max exclaimed. "How did you do that?"

"Long story, come on!" Liliana pulled Max out of the cell and through the corridor.

"Where is he?" Max asked, looking around them.

"That wore off fast," Liliana said. Sentinel was up and about already, and he was nowhere to be seen. Liliana almost fired off another sedative as a figure came racing around the corner ahead of them.

"Hurry! We don't have long left," Yates shouted at them, turning to run back the way they came. Liliana and Max ran after them. Could they make it out without another fight?

Chapter Thirty

"Maxie," a voice called behind them. They turned to see Sentinel step out of a cell behind them, but he wasn't alone. The three of them skidded to a halt to turn and face Sentinel, who was holding Rose by the throat in front of him.

"Rose!" Liliana couldn't help but shout. "You let her go," she ordered Sentinel, who just laughed in response.

"You played dirty first, Ana," Sentinel replied.

"Don't call me that," Liliana replied. Something about what he said was niggling at the back of her mind. She locked eyes with Rose. She was scared but she was staring Liliana down. She seemed to be trying to tell her something while saying nothing. A moment later, it all clicked together.

"Timmy," Liliana said simply. His angry response all but confirmed her suspicion.

"What?" Max asked, looking between them. "You have got to be joking me." He looked both relieved and annoyed to have the mystery of Sentinel's secret identity made clear.

"Alright. Fair enough, that was a slipup, I'll admit it," Tim replied, clearly annoyed at himself. "Anyway, it's not like any of you are going to make it out of here to tell anyone." He tightened his grip on Rose's throat and she pulled at his hand in response.

"Let her go!" the three of them shouted at him, each preparing to fight.

"Or what?" Sentinel taunted them, lifting Rose off the floor to show off his strength.

"Coming through," a voice called behind them. Liliana and Max stepped apart just at the right time for Johnathon to come running through. He didn't stop. He tucked his head in and aimed straight for Tim's torso. Tim thought nothing of the attack. But then again, he didn't know about Johnathon's power. The shock that hit Tim's face as Johnathon knocked him flying was beautiful to behold. He quickly let go of Rose, who dropped to the floor. Tim continued to go flying backwards, hard enough to hit his head on the doorframe at the end of the corridor and collapse to the floor.

"Did you just knock him out with one hit?" Liliana asked Johnathon, astonished that it worked that well. She looked over at Tim, noting the blood running down the side of his head. Not much, but enough to show Johnathon's strength.

"Apparently," Johnathon replied, helping Rose up from the floor. "Are you okay?" Johnathon lowered his helmet, showing his face to the woman who believed him dead.

"Johnny? How on earth are you alive?" Rose asked.

"Long story," Liliana and Yates replied at the same time.

"Superpowers can come in useful, apparently," Johnathon replied with a shrug.

"I wouldn't believe you have powers if you hadn't just sent Sentinel flying with a headbutt right now," Rose replied.

"There will be time for chatting later. We need to move," Yates ordered the group. Max was quiet as they ran back through the prison towards the garage, to their freedom. As they passed the corridor where Liliana and Yates had split up, she noticed some fire damage to the walls. She needed to ask Yates what happened there once they were out of the prison.

Liliana could hear struggling in the security office; the guards had woken up. "Faster!" she shouted at the group. They needed to pick up the pace before the guards on the outside got word of what had happened. Together they ran down the stairwell and squished themselves into the van. Yates and Rose sat up front with the camouflage screen still active, hiding the three in the back.

Yates pulled the van out of the underground car park and back down the long drive out of the prison.

"What do we do now?" Max asked. He did not know what they were planning, simply putting his life into their hands.

"Shh," Liliana told him to be quiet. They needed to sneak past security still. She was practically sitting on Max's lap in the back of the van, not that she truly minded, of course. It felt good to be this close to him again.

"Hold on," Johnathon said, squatting next to them, computer open on his knees. "Here's something I made earlier." He smiled as he activated a piece of software embedded in the prison security system. It opened both the gates giving Yates the space to speed up and race through the open gates.

"Nicely done." Liliana praised Johnathon's work as she opened the partition between the group, the road open before them. "Do you think we can make it back to base before Sentinel wakes up?"

"It doesn't matter. He's got bigger problems right now," Yates replied, smirking in the driver's seat.

"What do you mean?" Max asked.

"His little outburst back there was being streamed to the entire world," Yates laughed. Neither Johnathon nor Liliana knew they had planned this.

"Seriously?" Liliana asked, joining in the celebration. "So, the whole world knows who he is?"

That would distract him from following them. He

would have no reason to follow them if his secret was out.

"Not only that, but they saw him hold a normal human as a hostage," Rose croaked, rubbing her neck where Tim had held her. "That's not going to look good for him."

"Are you actually trying to tell me you broke me out of prison, and took down Sentinel, all in one morning?" Max asked, finding the truth hard to believe.

"Well, it was a team effort that took a lot of planning," Liliana replied. "It's not as simple as that. Plus, we wouldn't have needed to do all of this if you had listened to Yates in the first place."

Max had the grace to look embarrassed by Liliana's words. His cheeks flushed as he admitted his mistakes.

"So, what now?" Max asked, trying to draw the attention away from his slipup.

"Now we go back to base and see what the world makes of the new footage we have shown them," Liliana replied as they made their way into the city. "Maybe now people will actually start to think for themselves."

"They might even start to question where these powers came from in the first place," Max added, glancing over at Johnathon, conflicted.

The footage from the prison was already streaming on screens on every street. The sun was rising behind them, dawning on a brand-new realisation for the city. That maybe, just maybe, they shouldn't put all their trust into a fallible superhero.

The end

About The Author

J.l. Meyrick

J.L. Meyrick can be found in the South West of England, with her husband and 2-year-old noise monster.

If she's not writing she can either be found chasing a toddler around her with her nose in a book.

You can follow her on various social medias;
Twitter - @JLMeyrickAuthor
TikTok - @AuthorJLMeyrick
Instagram - @JLBarrett_Writer

Or you can sign up to her newsletter for all the latest info on new releases.

Books By This Author

The Revelation Academy

The Apocalypse is coming.

What is Olivia going to do when faced with the reality of the end of the world? Transported into a world of warfare and teenage drama. New friends mix with enemies as Olivia figures out her place in a growing, and fighting, world.

Printed in Great Britain
by Amazon